112

Tell Me No Secrets

Tell Me No Secrets

Nikki-Michelle

Urban Books, LLC
78 East Industry Court
Deer Park, NY 11729

ISBN 13: 978-1-62090-176-2

Printed in the United States of America

*This is a work of fiction. Any references or similarities
to actual events, real people, living, or dead, or to real
locales are intended to give the novel a sense of reality. Any similarity in other names, characters, places,
and incidents is entirely coincidental.*

Tell Me No Secrets

Nikki-Michelle

Dedication

For Michelle and Sam, and to Kai Leakes, one day may my pen be as great as yours.

Aric

My already unpleasant mood had gotten even worse by the time I'd pulled up to my house. My wife's car was parked in the cul-de-sac and she knew I hated that shit. Why didn't she park in the garage like I asked? I'd known why. It was to annoy me. She got off on annoying me. I wondered how long it had taken her father's power and privilege to get her out of jail. After she had shown her ass at my job and attacked Chyanne there was nothing I could do to keep her from getting arrested. And to keep my job, I'd had to get on damage control immediately. Don't get me wrong, my wife's being locked up bothered me, but not as much as losing the position in the company after I'd worked so hard to get everything going the way I'd wanted.

Then, there was Chyanne I had to worry about. By the time I had gotten to the office they'd told me she was already gone and had given her resignation letter. Dealing with all of that and trying to convince the board that everything was just one big misunderstanding was a task in itself. Then, to find out a couple of days later that Chyanne was pregnant had me running in circles. I'd known there would be a lot of questions and believe me there would be some answers, but first things first. I needed to deal with my wife.

I had just left the hospital arguing with Chyanne about getting a DNA test and I knew all hell was waiting for me on the other side of my kitchen door as I parked my Navigator. My wife's car was parked angry, like she had just whipped it into that spot and had left it there without thought. Before I could turn my key in the knob to unlock the door, she snatched it open. She did it with such force that the wind she created blew the jet black hair from her round exotic face.

"That's the fat bitch you messing around on me with this time, Aric?" Venom was laced in her cat like voice.

Stephanie had the kind of voice that drove a man mad in the bedroom, but, in an argument, could cut you like the sharpest machete. I brushed past her and threw my keys on the bar as I walked into the kitchen.

A picture fell from the wall when she slammed the door.

As I looked at my wife in her hazel and green eyes, I could tell she had been in a fight and had obviously lost. Her eyes were swollen, bottom lip was busted, and bruises were visible on the right side of her jaw. There were scratches that surrounded her neck like they were some exotic tattoo, a splint covered her left wrist and a Band Aid was over her right eye.

"Still starting fights you can't win I see," I said to her before taking a swallow from the bottle of water in my hand.

As soon as she started across the room, I'd known she was coming to get physical. So, I made a move to grab her before she could. I caught the hand she was aiming to slap me with, shoving her away from me. She quickly caught her balance and picked up the butcher's knife she had obviously already planted.

"Go ahead and try that shit today, Aric, and one of us will go to hell and the other to jail," she spat as she stood in a defensive posture that she had no doubt learned from years of kickboxing training.

I threw the water bottle down. "I've told you about putting your damn hands in my face. Now you try that shit and you are going to eat that fucking knife."

"Sick of you cheating on me, Aric."

"Give me a divorce like I asked and you won't have this problem."

"No. Ti'l death do us part. We both said for better or worse . . ."

We were at a standstill, just like our marriage had been for the last two years. She dropped the knife and ran her fingers through her hair.

"Obviously whoever wrote that shit didn't know you would be taking the vows," I snapped back.

"I don't understand why you want to divorce me," her voice cracked. "With all of the things that we've been through, Aric, everything, and you want to divorce me? What happened? I thought we were going to work this out. Is she the reason you don't call like you used to? Is she the reason why you asked me to stay back in New York and give you space?"

"She has a name. Her name is Chyanne and you know damn well we've had this problem before I came to Atlanta."

She frowned and cocked her head to the side. "Please, don't tell me you're standing here defending your mistress to me! You need to fire her—"

Now it was my time to frown. "What?"

Even if Chyanne hadn't quit, I wouldn't have fired her.

"Fire her. You can't very well think I am going to be okay with her still working in that office with you."

Her voice was following behind me because I had brushed past her and was making my way up the stairs to my bedroom. As I loosened my tie she kept on with her useless tirade.

"Aric, don't ignore me! I don't understand—"

"You don't understand what? What part of a divorce do you not understand? It's over and done. It's been that way for a long time now. Chyanne had nothing to do with that."

"Will you stop defending that slut?" She lashed out at me and jumped in my face right as I pulled my shirt off.

I grabbed her by both arms and moved her away from in front of me. "She's done nothing to you, so why are you attacking her?"

She looked incredulous. "She's done nothing to me? She's fucking my husband?" she yelled out.

"I wouldn't be your husband if you would've signed the divorce papers when you were supposed to."

I gently shoved her on the bed and walked toward the bathroom to shower. The day had been long for me and all I wanted to do was sleep. I'd been doing so much to try to get the office back in order and to try and get Chyanne to agree to give me a DNA test that all I wanted to do at the moment was relax. Chyanne was the woman I'd been cheating on my wife with. She used to be my executive assistant and I hadn't set out to have sex with her. But, there was something about Chyanne that attracted me to her and made me want to take it there. Somehow, my wife put two and two together and showed up at my office asking questions. I figured that someone in the office had told her what they all had been suspecting, that it was Chyanne I'd been seeing. That was all she needed to hear to act an ass and attack Chyanne. I never told Chyanne I was married because, to be honest, I wasn't planning on still being married.

Those thoughts quickly filtered away when I felt Stephanie's nails dig into my back and her fist pound the back of my head. That type of BS was the thing I was sick of. My wife had a really nasty habit of putting her hands on me.

"The fuck is wrong with you?" I yelled at her before turning, grabbing her by her wrists, and violently shaking her.

Her hair shook wildly around her face when she fell back on the bed. She tried to jump up and I pushed her back down on the bed, harder than I did the first time. Standing over her, I held her down by her wrists, sick of doing that same song and dance with her.

"You're hurting me, Aric."

I knew I was hurting her wrists with the pressure I was putting on them, but it seemed the only way I could get her to act right was to put my hands on her in some way.

"I'm done fighting with you Stephanie. Done. We are done. Sign the damn papers and let go," I said to her through clenched teeth.

She squirmed wildly still trying to get away from me as she screamed at me. "No Aric. You will not throw away twenty years of what we have built for some new piece of ass."

"You know damn well, she has nothing to do with this. Stephanie, how long have we been playing this game? How long have I been asking you for a divorce? It was long before Chyanne came about."

"You're lying. Everything was fine until you started to change again. I knew it was somebody else. I knew it. I knew as soon as you came to Atlanta that there would be some BS all over again. And then when I called you yesterday and the day before, you were all pissed off. It's like your attitude changed overnight. Is that why you asked me to stay in New York? Is she the one that I always hear in the background asking who I am? Why? Why Aric? You're going to walk away from all we have together?"

She was belligerent. Screaming, crying, and yelling. The day she'd attacked Chyanne in the office, I hadn't even known she was in town until I'd gotten a phone call from Gabe telling me that some mess was about to go down because Stephanie was at my office. Obviously, I hadn't made it in time enough to stop what'd happened between her and Chyanne.

Now, we wrestled. Well she wrestled around trying to punch, kick, and scratch my hand to make me release my grip. Tears started to fall down her face as fought against my strength. After she'd tired herself out, she just looked up at me and I looked down at her hoping she would be calm enough for me to let her go. My back was burning like hell and I no longer desired to go to sleep in the same house with her.

"Are you okay now?" I asked her as calmly as I could.

She nodded, so I slowly released her and stood straight up but I wasn't fool enough to turn my back on her again. I looked around the room searching for my shirt.

"Where're you going?" she asked me when she saw me pull my white T-shirt back over my head.

"Out."

She jumped up, quick as lightning, and blocked my way out before she threw herself against me and wrapped her arms around my neck.

"Please, don't go. Don't leave me, Aric. I know I've messed up a lot when it's come to us but, baby, I can change. I can. You know I can."

She was begging and pleading like she had done several times over the last couple of years. When she'd done this little routine before, I had fallen for it many times hoping that, maybe, our marriage would last. I'd wished that we could push past all that had happened between us, but there had been no such luck. No matter how many times we had tried, we always came back to the same point, always having to start back at step one.

I didn't even have to look down at her to know that she was still crying. "Stephanie, stop," I said to her as I tried to pull her arms from around my neck.

She stood on her toes and placed kisses against my face, neck, and mouth as she pleaded with me to stay with her.

"We can fix this," she pleaded again. "I'll forget about this one. We can move past her. I won't bring her up again. Right now, we can start over. We can start fresh, whatever you want. Just don't leave me."

I exhaled and my eyes rolled as my head fell back and I let out an exasperated breath. I reached up and grabbed her hands, finally removing her from around my neck. Too much had happened between Stephanie and me. Too many fights, too many cases of infidelity, and too many chances to fix what had been broken for so long.

"This can't be fixed," I said as I looked in her eyes, hoping she would feel and get what I was saying to her.

"Yes it can, Aric. I know she doesn't mean anything to you. She's just another one of your little adventures. I can get past that. We can get past it and we can move on."

"There is no moving on," I yelled at her.

She cried harder and tried to come back to hug me. I pushed her off of me and she tried harder to get me to hug her, kiss her.

"Stephanie, stop. Please, stop. You're just making it worse."

"Please don't tell me you are going to leave me for this young bitch. What does she have that I don't? I'm your wife. I have been your wife for fifteen damn years. We have been together for twenty years! All of that history you're going to walk away from for—"

"This has nothing to do with her."

I yelled at her, frustrated that she was trying to make this about Chyanne, knowing that it wasn't. Gently pushing her out of my way, I made my way downstairs to the kitchen so I could get to my keys.

"Yes, it does. I know it does. If you cared so much about her then why did you come to New York and why did we make love like we did? If you really wanted to leave me, then why, Aric? Why did you continue to tell me you loved me? Why did you hold me the way you did when we were in bed together?"

I shook my head and went to pick up my keys from the bar, but she quickly grabbed them before I could.

"Don't go. Stay so we can talk about this," she pleaded. "None of the women you have cheated on me with have been able to hold your attention for long. You always come back baby. So, when you get that fat bitch out of your system, I, your wife, will still be here. I know you will tire of her soon and when you do, we can talk. When she is out of the picture—"

"She'll never be out of the picture," I said to her as my mind went back to Chyanne at the hospital.

I looked up at Stephanie just in time to see the hate flitter across her eyes.

"What?" she barely got out above an angry whisper.

I waited a second before answering her, knowing what I was about to say would hurt her way worse than me cheating on her. I folded my arms across my chest before deciding to continue on.

"She'll never be out of the picture," I repeated. "She's pregnant."

My words stunned her to the point that she dropped down almost lifelessly on the sitting stool behind her, dropping my keys back on the bar. She sat there and just stared at the wall in front of her before slowly turning back to look at me. Tears slowly fell down her face again. At first there was raw pain written on her face then there was unmitigated anger.

"So. . . . you're going to make her have an abortion right?" she asked me as she slowly spun around on the stool to face me directly. "Right, Aric? She's having an abortion, right?"

"No. I'm not making her have an abortion."

Old pain that I hadn't felt in years gripped me and put a smirk on my face when she stood and faced the wall. Her back showed she was huffing and puffing. I was prepared for her rage when she turned back to face me.

"Four," she started as she held up the same amount of fingers. "Four abortions I have had. Three I had because you asked me to because you said we didn't need kids at that time. And now. . . . now, you're telling me you want to have a child with a woman you barely even know?"

"Let's get this shit right," I countered as I pressed my palms down on the bar and leaned forward. "I asked you to have two abortions because we were both in college and didn't need kids right then. One was because you'd decided you weren't ready and one you did to hurt me. Well guess what? It worked. You knew I wanted that baby. You knew I wanted a child more than anything I had ever wanted up until that moment. When you told me you had killed my child, you did so with a look of satisfaction on your face. You took my child's life only to hurt me."

"Because, you had hurt me, Aric. Plenty of times you'd hurt me."

"So you paid me back by killing my child?"

Our voices were elevated and I'm sure if the neighbors had listened closely they could have heard us. I was prepared for her to have a snappy comeback, but she simply shook her head and covered the tears falling rapidly down her face.

"I was wrong. I know that, but don't throw this baby in my face Aric. Make her get rid of it . . ."

"It? It? She's carrying my seed. Not a damn, 'it'."

"Aric, please do not throw this child in my face. You know this ain't right," she said.

She slowly stood and looked at me.

There was silence between us. Although I didn't want to admit it, it hurt me to see her hurting. Stephanie and I had weathered a lot together and I'd known Chyanne's pregnancy would break her, but in no way would I tell her that I believed there was a chance this baby wouldn't be mine. I wanted her to hurt the way she had hurt me.

"A lot of things we've done ain't been right, but that has never stopped you before has it? It is what it is," I said to her as I snatched my keys up and made my way out of door.

She yanked the door back to keep it from closing and followed me to the car.

"You will not be flaunting another baby around in my face," she said.

I got in my car and slammed the door closed.

She kicked the door and slapped her open palms against the window. I ignored her.

"You'd better make her get rid of it, because if you don't . . . I will."

I heard her yell that at me as I continued to ignore her and backed out of the driveway, not caring how she felt about it.

Chyanne

When the doctors came into my room five days after I had arrived at the hospital and told me I could go home, I was so happy. I wanted to jump up out of that bed and run for the door. I was so glad to get the catheter out of me so I could urinate naturally that I didn't know what to do. I'd only been stuck to that bed for almost a week but it had felt like forever. I quickly stood after the nurses were done with the drawing of my blood and taking my blood pressure. All I wanted to do was go home and get in my bed. My body had gone through a lot in the past week and my mental capacity was on overload. For the first few nights lying in that bed, all that kept playing through my head was Aric hitting me.

When he'd come to my house after Jamie showed up at the office for my birthday and kissed me in front of everyone, he'd found the pictures that Jamie had taken of me. I hadn't thought to put the pictures away because I didn't expect the events of that day to go down as such. Needless to say Aric got to my house before I did and found the pictures which led to him putting his hands on me.

I couldn't get the images of the bruises on my face and body out of my head. I'd cried myself to sleep or cried until a headache put me to sleep. Over and over I wanted what had happened to be one bad dream because I didn't want Aric to be married and I didn't want to be pregnant with a married man's baby. I didn't want to be in love with a married man. The hardest thing for me to do was to realize that I had been a fool and had been played like a game of chess. I never thought I'd see the day when I had to fight another woman about her husband, especially when I didn't even know he was married to begin with.

I looked at my phone vibrating on the bed and saw that it was Aric. I blew out steam as all of the emotions came flooding back, almost causing tears to fall from my eyes. I really didn't want to be bothered with him, but since my car was at home, I had no choice. I had no one else to call. Aric and I had been arguing non-stop since I had been in the hospital. He wanted to do a paternity test when it was quite obvious that I was too high risk to have one before the baby was born. I didn't know why he was acting stupid. He knew he was the only man I'd been sleeping with around the time I got pregnant, which meant I was already pregnant when I'd had sex with Jamie. Speaking of which, he had been calling me too. I liked Jamie . . . liked him a lot, just didn't know what to do about it since I was in love with Aric and now pregnant with his baby. I knew I had to tell Jamie about my pregnancy and that would mean that whatever it was that we had established would have to stop. I didn't want any mess with Aric on that. He was already acting stupid enough.

I pulled on the terry cloth sweat suit Aric had brought up for me the day before and slid my feet into casual Polo sneakers. Just as I was putting the last of my clothing into the gym bag he had bought me, he opened the door.

"You ready?" he asked me as he closed the door behind him.

"Yeah. Just need to wait for the discharge papers," I answered.

"Damn, they couldn't have already had that ready?"

I side eyed him as I walked in front of the mirror to fix my hair and stopped cold in my tracks. Although the bruises were not as bad as they once were, they were still there. All that had happened before my trip to the hospital came flooding back to the fore front of my mind. Tears threatened to fall, but I quickly pulled myself together as I brushed my hair into a ponytail and caught Aric's eyes in the mirror.

"We need to talk," he said to me.

That we did, I thought as I watched him while finishing my ponytail. He stood there with his hands in his pockets and I could tell he had been at work. His hazel eyes watched me behind his glasses as he licked his lips. The reminder of what he could do with those lips subtle, but it made me appreciate the thickness of them. He had on his signature Armani suit in dark gray with thin white pin stripes. As usual he had the vest to match with a tie that complimented the suit and a crisp white dress shirt underneath it. His muscle defined shape could be made out behind the suit. Dark gray shoes, which I could bet money were Armani as well, set the whole ensemble.

I didn't comment as I grabbed my purse and my bag. He quickly took the bag away from me and I didn't want to be that close to him. His eyes gave me the once over and those same feelings that had made me fall for him the first time around smacked me in the face. Standing that close to him made me feel the same weakness I had felt for him whenever he was near me. I made a big deal of putting my phone in my purse and was happy when the doctor finally came into the room with the discharge papers.

I listened to her tell me about the prenatal vitamins and iron pills she had prescribed and I paid close attention because, believe it or not, being pregnant scared me badly. I didn't even think I knew how to be a mother. The last thing she told me was that I was on strict bed rest. That meant that most of my day should be spent in bed. I cast a quick glance at Aric from time to time and I could see that he was paying as much attention as I was. When she was finished with her instructions we walked out of my room and it was amazing how many women were willing to nearly trip over themselves looking at him. I simply shook my head; if they only knew what I knew.

We were barely out of the parking lot before his phone started blowing up. I assumed it was his wife. For some reason I wanted to reach over and slap him for all the mess he had put me through knowing full well the whole time he was married. There was a surge of jealousy that overtook me. It made me feel some type of way to know that for the last few days it was possible that he had been home with her, holding her, kissing her, making love to her. It had me wondering if he did to her what he'd done to me. My fist clenched and I found myself wanting to lash out at him. I was surprised by my anger, but why should I be? He had played me and played me well! Sitting in his truck beside him I felt like a fool, a complete idiot!

"Why didn't you tell me you were married, Aric?"

Forget waiting to talk, I thought.

He quickly looked at me before licking his lips and turning his eyes back to the road. We would have to leave the hospital when there was a lot of traffic and congestion.

"Does that even matter? You know now."

I furrowed my brow and turned in my seat to look at him. He couldn't be serious.

"Say what? Aric you had me running around here for months thinking that whenever you fixed what you said you had to fix that we would be together. And you knew all of this damn time that you were married," I retorted. "You could at least say, 'I'm sorry'."

I had turned my back to the passenger side window and was using my hands to talk and get my point across.

"Look, Chyanne, I could apologize for it, but would that make you feel any better about it? Would that make it any less painful than it is?"

I watched the muscles flex in his right arm underneath his shirt as he gripped the stirring wheel.

"Maybe not, but an apology would be nice. I didn't want to be your mistress Aric or anyone's for that matter. I feel like a damn fool," I said. "And then to be attacked by the woman when I didn't even know who she was takes the cake don't you think?"

"That, I will apologize for. I had no idea she would do that."

"Well what in hell would you expect? I was sleeping with the husband I didn't know she had."

All he did was cut his eyes at me. Those eyes still sent chills through me even though I was mad and didn't want them to. I quickly turned and looked out of the passenger side window. There was a family in a neon blue PT Cruiser beside us and two children, a boy and a girl, were in the back laughing and clapping as the mother was clapping her hands and singing. The father had the biggest smile on his face like his family was all that mattered. I smiled when the little girl turned to me and waved. I waved back and she went back to singing with her mother, brother, and father. I could only think about how I'd wished my childhood would've been that jubilant. My childhood had been filled with nothing but nightmares that I prayed to God and hoped my child would never have to endure.

Once we pulled into my driveway, I allowed Aric to help me down from his truck. I was tired and I was starving. *That hospital food had done nothing for me*, I thought, as I listened to him talk on his phone to whoever his new assistant was. I must admit that it made me jealous that he had already replaced me. Made me wonder if he was doing to her in his office what he had done to me. Whoever she was, she obviously wasn't as good as I was because he was fussing at her about something she had done to erase the files he had left on her desk.

I minded my business and checked my messages. Justin had called me several times. I expected him to. He'd been the only real friend I had in the office. I played several messages he had left.

"Okay bitch! Imma put out a APB on your ass if you don't call me today. I came by your house today and the neighbors told me last they had seen you were being carted off by an ambulance. I done called Southern Regional, Grady, Emory, Atlanta Medical, and Henry Medical. Henry said they had somebody by your name but couldn't release any information. Bitch you got twenty-four hours ta call me or I will do just what I said. Bye. Love you girl. I pray that you are safe!"

I laughed at Justin. He and I had been friends since we'd both started at B&G a little over four years ago. He had the gayest of the queen's voices and it sounded like a mixture between Ru Paul and Wendy Williams. The last message he had left was six hours ago. I got a few messages from Jo-Jo, Aaron, and Aaden, and a few more people from work had called. The call from April's sons made my mind wander to her and think of the mess we had made of our friendship. To think she'd intentionally gone after Aric simply because she'd known I liked him still grated my nerves.

Although what she had done was wrong on so many levels, I found myself missing the friendship we'd had. She was the only person I could call a friend. Getting back to checking the messages I noticed Gabriel had called me but I quickly stopped playing his message and turned my machine off when Jaime's voice popped up.

"You ready to talk now?" Aric asked from behind me and almost made me jump out of my skin.

I turned to him and nodded before I followed his lead to my front room. He took the loveseat and I took the sofa.

"Looks like we may be having a baby coming soon," he started.

I smacked my lips and rolled my eyes at the *may be* part.

"I don't really care how you feel about it, until we get DNA it will always be a possible, maybe," he said again.

"Aric, did you not hear that woman say I was twelve to thirteen weeks pregnant? You were the first man I ever had sex with twelve to thirteen weeks ago," I said, annoyance clearly laced in my voice. I propped one leg under me and plopped down on the sofa again.

"I don't know that," he countered.

"You have some nerve. Are you calling me a whore?" Both my brows raised as I stared pointedly at him.

"I'm saying that I saw you fucking another man. The same man that was in my damn office building with gifts and shit tonguing you down on your birthday! Say what you want, until I get the blood work, it is what it is."

I didn't even know what to say to that. He had been having sex with April, whoever else, he had a wife, and he wanted to act like this with me?

"I guess that means I should be asking you to see your HIV status and such huh?" I asked.

"What?"

The look on his face was skeptical as if he couldn't believe I had just asked him that question.

"You're asking me for a DNA test and I am asking you about your status. You were having sex with me, April, your wife, and only God knows who else, so proof of your status would be nice to go along with my proof of paternity."

"Kiss my ass, Chyanne! You weren't asking for any of that shit when my dick was inside of you. You didn't care about any of that when my face was in your pussy either. So fuck what you're talking about and get me a DNA test then we can talk."

I cringed at his choice of words. He was always so brash and I was not about to sit and go tit for tat with him.

"You'll get your DNA test when I get my info on your status," I said as I stood to walk to my bathroom hoping that he wouldn't get mad enough to come behind me.

I needed and wanted a long hot shower. Being in that hospital had me feeling like I wasn't fully clean. So many things were running through my mind. I wanted to ask a lot of questions about him and his wife, but I didn't want him to evade the questions. Knowing him, he would answer a question with a question. I guess the first thing I needed to do was to calm down because I was so worked up. As I tried to walk past him, Aric grabbed my wrist and pulled me down onto his lap. My nerves shot up and my body overheated. I inhaled and exhaled with my eyes closed biting down on my lip to contain my emotions as his arms enclosed around my waist.

"I really don't want to play this game with you Aric. I really don't." I heard my voice crack so I knew he had heard it too.

"What game?" he asked.

His voice had dipped an octave and it was working every nerve ending in my body right along with the way his eyes gazed over my face. It would have done me some good not to forget what this man had done to me.

"Aric, you are a married man and you've hurt me enough in these last past couple of months to last me a lifetime."

"Okay, look. You're right. I've hurt you. I know that, but if this baby is mine, we will always be a part of each other's lives. You have to get used to that."

"That, I can deal with. What I can't have is you thinking that it will be more than that. I can't carry on a relationship with a married man and I definitely can't have you putting your hands on me when you feel like it. I can't do that Aric and I won't."

I quickly closed my eyes again to fight off his energy.

"Check this out," he began. "I'm not making excuses for my behavior. I know I've got some things that I need to fix and I know what I've done to you is wrong, but me apologizing for it isn't going to erase your pain or make you forget it, so what's the use?"

I opened my eyes and turned to look at him. "No an apology won't erase it, but at least I'll know you feel some sympathy about what you've done."

He licked his lips as he tilted his head to the side and quirked an eyebrow at me. The cocky disposition wasn't lost on me as I made my way to my bathroom. I was not about to go through the motions with him anymore than I had to. He had kept me on a string for months with this no title thing he was pushing around knowing full well he was married and had no intentions on taking this any further than where it had gone. My anger level shot up another notch as I turned the shower on and adjusted the water temperature.

I stood there for a minute and thought about my mother. Why had she done it? Why had she stayed with a man who'd treated her the way my father had? What had made her stay there day after day, month after month, year after year? What kind of hold had my father had on her that'd made her want to stay with him and be his punching bag? The things I'd seen, no child should have had to see. No child should've had to see their mother being dragged, kicked, and punched. I hated my father and I would forever hate him until the day I died. Hate's a strong word, but that's how I felt at that moment. Sometimes I hated my mother; hated her for allowing me to be subjected to such a broken home. I hated her for allowing woman after woman to disrespect her marriage and then to have my father act as if it was his God given right to have a wife and however other many women he'd wanted to have. I would not live my life that way. I refused to.

I'd gotten out of my clothes and had one foot in the shower when I snatched my robe on and walked back into my front room. Aric was on the phone and it was apparent from the snippet I'd heard he was talking to his wife. In a sense I felt bad for her, but then I kept remembering she sucker punched me and fought with me about her husband. He looked up at me when I stood in front of him. I balled my fists in anger and my patience was gone.

"Let me call you back," he said into the phone and hung up before he could get a response.

"You are not going to sit in my house and disrespect me again. You want to talk to your wife then you do it outside and off my property," I snapped.

I could tell he was surprised by the way his brows raised.

"I am not playing with you, Aric," I snapped again as I slapped his hand when he reached for my waist. I walked over to my front door and snatched it open. "I want you to leave right now. I need to be alone."

The cold air reminded me that I had no clothes on under the robe I was wearing. He stood slowly and made his way to the door.

"So that's how it is between us now?"

I let go of the door and pulled my robe tighter when he got too close for comfort.

"Yes, Aric. That's how it is. I'm no longer going to play this game with you. I have a child to think about and . . ."

I stopped talking and backed away a bit when he closed the gap between us and tried to avert my eyes when he used his finger to lift my face to his.

"I'll be back tomorrow so we can talk about what we are going to do about this child you're carrying. If it's mine, get used to me being around because I won't be going anywhere."

I noticed he had put emphasis on the word *we* both times he'd said it and was mentally thrown off balance when he brought his lips to mine and kissed me. I didn't know what to do or think. I wasn't prepared for him to do that and was mad at myself for letting him pull me close to him, deepening the kiss.

"See you tomorrow," he said before turning and walking out of the door. "Lock the door behind me. I want to hear you lock it so I'll know it's locked. Get some rest and we'll talk tomorrow."

I nodded, closed the door, and locked it. Shaking my head and thinking about what had just happened I made my way back to the shower. Stepping into the shower I silently thanked God that the water hadn't turned cold. I stood there a while and let the hot water wash over my back. That hospital bed hadn't been my friend when it had come to my back. I cringed when I turned around and the water hit my sensitive nipples. Quickly washing myself, I finished up, oiled myself down, and crawled into bed.

There was a lot that I needed to think about. A lot I had to do. A sudden feeling washed over me; one minute I was scared to the point of tears that I was about to become a mother, and then the next minute I was jubilant thinking that God had blessed me with a chance to show the world that I could be a good mother. I was a ball of emotions all night, even as I talked on the phone with Justin and told him about all of the madness. He had wanted to come over and sit with me but I declined, stating that I wanted to be alone. I promised him that we could get together the following week and after worrying myself to death about being a mother, being pregnant by a married man, and being in love with a married man, I prepared myself for a sleepless night.

Aric

Niki Michelle

"Wow! So she's pregnant?" Gabriel asked me, shock written across his face.

It was Monday afternoon and we were in my entertainment room that had come custom built with the house. Three forty-two-inch flat screen TVs lined the wall as well as a movie theater style screen on the back wall. The left side of the room housed a bar that made the room appear more like a sports bar with a theater-style setting. The stained concrete floors and stoned wall gave it a masculine feel and the red and black leather sofas and chairs gave off a laid-back mood.

I nodded and took another swig of my Corona before racking the balls up for another round of pool. I'd won the last one. "Yes sir! Asked her for a DNA test though because like I told you, I saw the pictures of her and ole boy."

Gabriel chuckled and sat down on the stool behind him. "Okay, this is what I don't get. You usually do your thing with these women and then you leave them alone. You treat Chy differently, like you want to be with her. Do you want to be with her? If not, I don't understand the possessive nature you have toward her. Doesn't make sense . . . ."

It wasn't lost on me that he called her Chy, like they had gotten close enough to have pet names for one another. I still hadn't let him know that I knew he'd taken her to lunch. I made my first shot before answering him and besides, I needed time to contemplate my answer.

"Has nothing to do with that. Chyanne is different. You know what I mean? She's a different breed. I know she's young, but she's got her shit together. She knows what she wants in life. She's a hell of a worker and she's got pussy that Jesus would have sinned for."

Thinking about being inside of her caused my manhood to stir around in my jeans.

Gabriel laughed out loud and the sound resounded in the closed off area. "Wow, Aric. You're a fool, man."

I laughed with him. "For real though, Chyanne is different for me. I mean . . . let me put it to you like this," I said to him talking with my hands standing my pool cue up in front of me. "Stephanie has a dominant personality. Chyanne is submissive. Stephanie will tell me to cook for my damn self. Chyanne cooks for me. Stephanie only asks me how my day is going when she wants to talk about something. Chyanne asks me how my day is going because she genuinely cares. Stephanie likes to take control when we're having sex or likes to tell me what she wants. Chyanne gives me her body like it's an empty canvas and I'm an artist free to do with it as I please. . . . See where I'm going with this?"

He nodded emphatically before speaking. "So Chy's giving you something completely opposite of what you have at home?"

I nodded. "Right and I kid you not being inside of Chyanne will have you caught up. I'm not even in my right mind when we're having sex. All I can think about is how much I don't want to come out! Shit, sometimes I don't think. I just feel."

"Well you did say she was a virgin, right? I would think it would have that affect if you know what I mean." he said, after I missed my last shot. He picked up his stick and started looking for a shot after he sat his beer down.

I nodded and picked up my beer again. "Yeah, but got damn. Like I said," I continued after chuckling a bit. "I don't know, man. Something about Chyanne just feels different."

"So, you're saying that you may want to be with her like that, then?"

I shook my head. "Nah. I still feel she is a little too young for me to ever really consider being with her. You know? I'm thirty-nine. She's twenty-five. Big difference. I don't think she's ready. I was the first man she had been with, sexually I mean."

I watched Gabriel take an angle shot and miss. "Damn. I can't believe I missed that," he said.

I couldn't believe it either. That was his best shot, but it opened up a way for me to beat him at the game his father had taught us.

"So, what are you going to do about Stephanie? You know she called me cursing me out. I don't think I have ever been called so many sons of bitches in my life."

Mentioning Stephanie brought my mood down as I positioned myself for a bank shot.

"I didn't even mean to put you in the middle of that," I said to him.

"Hey, it is what it is right? All I'm asking is that you do the right thing by both her and Chy. You and Steph have history and Chy is a good girl."

"How do you know she's a good girl?"

"I mean, come on Aric. I used to call your office almost every day to speak with you about something or the other. Chy answered the phone enough for me to have established that she is a good woman with a good heart. Not to mention the few times you've brought her out to business socials. She's a good girl," he said talking with his hands.

"A good girl, with some great pussy."

He laughed again although I knew he was trying to be serious. In college he was the only man on campus who could get a woman to fuck just by laughing. He and I continued to play pool and joke around. He lost the last game and called it quits. A few hours had passed and we were busy watching Sports Center and talking trash about who was going to the Super Bowl and I couldn't help but to mention how good Chyanne's sex was again when Stephanie walked in. I turned to look at her quickly before turning back to the TV.

"What's up Steph?" Gabe spoke to her.

She didn't respond. For them to be brother and sister, their relationship was a funny one. They both had different mothers and the same father. Gabriel's mother was their father's mistress back in the day. Stephanie never let Gabe live that down, but he didn't seem to care one way or the other.

"Aric, may I speak to you for a minute?" she asked.

I turned to look at her as she stood with her hands on her hip. I could tell she had been to the salon because of the way her hair cascaded around her shoulders.

"I'm busy," I answered and turned back to watch the TV.

"You weren't too busy to be talking about how good some pussy was and you're only watching TV. This will only take a minute."

"Can't you see I have company?" I answered her without even turning around to look at her.

"You call this bastard company?"

It seemed as if she lived to throw snide remarks at Gabriel. He was a good one because I would have told her a thing or two about herself a long time ago, sister or no sister. Some of the things she'd said to him had made even my ass itch so I knew he had wanted to say something a time or two, but Gabe was a southern gentlemen and he didn't believe in disrespecting women.

"That's okay Aric. I was leaving anyway," he said as he tossed the empty beer bottle in his hand in the trashcan beside him.

I stood with him. We gave each other dap and the handshake to let others know we had pledged the purple and gold.

"I'll catch up with you later and don't forget about the meeting tomorrow. This will be big if we can get that merger deal on the table," I said to him.

"I'll be there. Talk to you then."

"Alright, man."

"Have a good day Stephanie," he said to her on his way out.

"Fuck off," was her response.

I turned the flat screens off and walked past her out of the room.

"Damn, Aric. Can't we at least have a civilized conversation?" she yelled at my back following me to the kitchen.

"You have to be talking to have a conversation Stephanie. You haven't said anything yet."

She threw her purse on the counter and swept her hair up into a ponytail before folding her arms across her chest. I started putting dishes into the dish washer and wiping down the counters. I didn't want to give her anything to start griping about. She was a neat freak and I really didn't feel like arguing with her about anything. I had too much on my mind. I had to deal with Chyanne later because she wanted to talk and I also had to get some proposals done for tomorrow. Too many other things were going on for me to get into a petty argument with her.

"How was your day?" she asked in a huff.

"Same ole, same ole," I answered.

I could tell she was trying her hardest to try and make conversation with me. She had been trying all weekend and I wouldn't say we talked like we used to do, but we talked.

"Would you like for me to cook dinner for you?"

I moved past her and threw the trash away. I shook my head. "No, I'll pick up something while I'm out."

"Oh you're going out tonight? On a Monday?"

In typical Stephanie fashion, she was trying to get me to give up information on my own instead of coming right out and asking. That was her thing.

"I have some business that I need to take care of. I'll be back when I'm done."

"What kind of business do you have to handle at—" she looked at her watch—"seven at night?"

"I have to go and talk to Chyanne about the baby," I told her, deciding to be as honest as I could in the situation.

She fidgeted around with the buttons on her shirt and I could tell by how her face had hardened that she was trying to choose her next words carefully.

"So, you're really going to let her keep this baby then?"

"Yes, Stephanie, I am."

I finished wiping down the counters, crossed one leg over the other at the ankles and waited for her response with my hands resting on the counter behind me.

"So what does that mean? For us, I mean?"

"Nothing's changed for us. I still want a divorce."

"Does that mean you are going to be with her? I mean, I know we've been having this fight about the divorce for almost two years now, but you have never been this adamant before. Do you love her?"

"No, I don't and this, the divorce, has nothing to do with her so stop trying to make it about her. This is our problem."

I watched what seemed like a wave of relief wash over her when hearing that I didn't love Chyanne. Guess that made her feel better.

"So there is no way for us to work this out? Twenty years gone just like that," she stated as she snapped her fingers to get her point across. "I love you Aric and I know that we have both done some fucked up things to one another, but please just think about this some more before you go through with this? You can't throw all we have away. We've built so much together."

By now she had walked closer to me and we were body to body as she looked up at me. Her hands were lightly gripping my shirt on each side and she was searching my eyes for some semblance of hope.

"Can we talk about this when I get back? Let me handle this thing with Chyanne tonight and when I get back, we can talk," I said to her.

Looking down at her, at that moment, I remembered a time when I was in love with her. There was a time when I would try to move heaven and earth to try and impress her, give her anything she wanted. There was a time when I wouldn't have thought of hurting her, had loved her too damn much to hurt her. Now, it was like she was an afterthought. I would do my dirt first and think about her later. So much had happened. I didn't know what we could do to fix a marriage that we both had done so much to destroy. At first Stephanie wanted a divorce as much as I, then all of a sudden, she changed her mind. I didn't know what had given her a change of heart, but it would take me some time to think about staying in a marriage that I felt was over.

Walking into T.G.I. Fridays made me realize I was hungry. I hadn't really had any real food all day and for some reason, Chyanne didn't want to meet at her house. I didn't argue with her. All I wanted her to do was agree to have the DNA test so I would know how I needed to proceed. The hostess led me to a section that had a mixture of chairs and a booth together that sat on the right hand side of the bar.

"Hello sir. My name is Rachel and I will be your server for the day. May I get you started with something to drink or an appetizer?" the waitress greeted, once she'd gotten to me.

I looked up at the waitress. "I'll take a Guinness, Foreign Extra Stout and the Jack Daniel burger with fries."

"Okay. No appetizers for you today?"

"No, and a glass of water please."

She nodded, took the menu, and walked off. My phone vibrated and I knew it was Chyanne before I even looked at the phone.

"Where are you?" I asked her.

"I'm coming in. Where are you sitting?"

"On the side of the bar in the booth nearest the kitchen."

"Okay." I could hear horns in the background and the wind blowing through her phone.

After she hung up the waitress came back with my beer. I only drank import beer. It was some of the purest and it fit my taste buds. Chyanne breezed in like a breath of fresh air and I would be lying if I said an easy smile didn't creep along my face. She did that for me. Chyanne relaxed me. Her hair was slicked back into a sleek ponytail and her skin glowed. She looked a whole lot better than she did last I left her. Now that I knew she was pregnant, I could tell. She sat in the chair and I stayed quiet until she finished with her order of a pecan crusted chicken salad and glass of water.

"Shouldn't you be eating more than that?" I asked her.

"If I could hold down more than that, I would. I can't hold any real food down. I'm sick all day and all I want to do is lay in bed and sleep. I throw up everything I eat, even crackers. So, I may not even eat the salad."

She said all of that while wiggling around in her chair trying to get comfortable.

"Why don't you move to the booth and let me take the chair?"

She stared at my wedding band before taking my outstretched hand and hopped down from the chair making her way to the booth. She seemed to be much more comfortable there. The waitress came back with her water right as I caught Chyanne staring at my wedding band again.

"Do you guys have Sprite or Ginger Ale?" she asked.

I could tell she'd copped an attitude and my guess is because she finally saw some semblance of me acknowledging that I was indeed married.

"Yes. Be right back," the waitress replied.

"What's with the papers?" Chyanne asked me, nodding toward my black leather carrying case.

"It's the information on prenatal DNA testing—"

Before I could finish she let out a sigh and shook her head. "You know I'm a high risk pregnancy Aric. Why can't this wait until after the baby is born?"

"Because, if this is my child, I want to know now. I don't want to play the waiting game."

"Well, isn't my word good enough for now? I wouldn't lie to you about this Aric. I know this baby is yours—"

"I don't know that Chyanne. Look, are you going to meet me halfway on this, or not? I have no problem doing what I'm supposed to do as a man for my child, if it's my child. However; my hands are tied until I know for sure if this baby is mine."

She rolled her eyes and snatched the papers. "I'll look over it. If this is going to cause too much stress to my body or the baby, you can forget about it until the baby is born."

I know many would think that I was being a selfish asshole by asking her to do the DNA test, but four of my children had been taken away from me. Two were of my own doing, I knew that, but the last child of mine that Stephanie killed was the one that had really gotten to me. That's the baby that I'd really wanted. When Stephanie had told me she was pregnant it was the greatest feeling in the world. Then to have her come home a week later and tell me she'd aborted it simply to hurt me was the worst fucking feeling a man could ever experience. So if Chyanne was carrying my child, I wanted to know for sure before I got excited about the notion of being a father again. Once I knew for sure, I could move forward.

By now the waitress had come back and was setting our food out before us. After all of that was settled and I had eaten the first bite of my burger, I looked up at her. She was slowly chewing on a piece of lettuce looking like she was about to be sick.

"Are you going to be okay over there?" I asked.

"Yeah, just feeling sick. Don't know why they call it morning sickness when it lasts all day long," she said as she turned the glass of water up and took a big swallow.

"Why don't we get this to go and get you home?"

I signaled for our waitress and asked her for the check and to go boxes. As I helped her to stand she looked like she was about to let up all she had swallowed. I quickly gave the waitress my card before looking back at Chyanne. She had a napkin over her mouth and before I could react she bolted toward the bathroom, but people were in her way so she turned and ran full throttle out of the front doors. Forgetting I had given the waitress my credit card, I ran after her. Once I got to her she was on the side of the building throwing up the little she had eaten. I walked up behind her and handed her the napkins I had picked up.

"Damn, why the hell do you keep trying to hold stuff down if you can't? They don't have any pills they can give you for that shit?" I asked her.

She snatched the napkins away from me and shook her head. "Not now Aric please."

"What? I'm just asking. There has to be something they can give you for that."

People were looking at us, more so because we both went running from the restaurant. I walked with Chyanne to her car, but quickly decided I would be driving her home when she stopped and had to regain her balance.

"Come on," I said to her as I took her keys from her hand.

"I'm fine Aric. I can drive myself home."

"Yeah, sure you can," I sarcastically replied as I opened the passenger side door and helped her into the car.

Making sure she was secure inside, I rushed back in to where we had been sitting, signed the receipt, left the waitress a tip, and retrieved our to-go bags. I made sure to ask the manager if I could leave my truck there until I could come back for it in a couple of hours. Adjusting Chyanne's driver seat to fit me comfortably, I drove her home. On the drive over we talked some more about the prenatal DNA test after I'd called Gabe and asked him if he would be able to pick me up and take me back to my car. She pretty much brushed me off, telling me she didn't feel like talking about it at that moment so I let it be. Once I helped her inside she wanted to shower so I waited around until she was out. There was a lot running through my mind at that moment. Part of me wanted to be excited at the notion that it was a possibility that I could be a father. The other part of me didn't want to get too excited about it and then be brought down when it was said not to be mine.

I looked at my phone as it rang. It was Stephanie. "Hello?"

"Where are you?" she asked.

"Dropping Chyanne off," I exhaled.

I could hear her moving around in the background. "She doesn't have a car?" Annoyance was clearly laced throughout her voice as well as accusation.

"Look, she got sick at the place we met and I drove her home. That's all."

She was silent for a second. "I guess." She exhaled. "When can I expect you home Aric?"

"I'll be home when I get there."

She chuckled a bit before asking, "So what does that mean Aric? You said we could talk when you came back home. I'll be waiting for your arrival soon. Don't make me come looking for you, and you know I will."

I hung up. I knew Stephanie was crazy enough to do something foul like that and the last thing I needed was for her to show up at Chyanne's house starting trouble. That's the thing with Stephanie at times she acted like my mother and that shit annoyed me more than anything. I called out to Chyanne as I stood and checked my watch. It was hard to see with the only lighting coming from a night light in her front room. I had heard the shower go off a few seconds before hanging up the phone. The door opened to the bathroom and I smelled the vanilla and ginger body wash she used waft up through my nose. I wasn't expecting her to come out with only a towel wrapped around her. My dick moved around in my pants a bit. Water dripped from her wavy hair and landed on her breast. Her eyes were cast at half mast and damn it if I didn't remember at that moment how it felt to be inside of her.

"You didn't have to stay Aric," she said in a tone that made my dick do a happy dance.

I don't know if she was doing it on purpose or not, but it had me a little excited. I watched her backside as she walked to the fridge and grabbed a bottle of water. Her thick thighs were glistening and just imagining what she tasted like had me licking my lips.

"I'm going to bed. You still have the keys so you can let yourself out," she said.

She tried to walk past me to her bedroom, but I caught her hand and stopped her, pulling her close to me.

"You miss me?" I asked her.

She didn't answer, only exhaled and looked down at the floor. As usual, I took my hand and lifted her chin to look at me.

"I don't feel well Aric and I want to go lay down."

She said that but I knew Chyanne and I knew her body. I could feel her shaking in my arms. That was all the answer I needed as I leaned down and kissed her soft plush lips. When she moaned and leaned in for the kiss, I deepened it. She'd missed me. My hands traveled down to grip her lush backside pulling her closer to me letting her feel my erection. She was holding on to my arms and her nails were threatening to break skin. Chyanne was a scratcher and I had the marks to prove it. I broke the kiss and turned her back to me, moving her hair to the side before kissing the base of her neck and down her spine to the point of where the towel stopped me. I reached around the front of her and removed her hand from the hold she had on the towel. It fell to the floor as I grabbed a handful of her breast. She hissed and told me they were sore as I kneeled down and planted kisses all over her back and derriere before standing and leading her over to the couch, pulling her down to straddle my lap.

I pulled her forward so I could taste her lips again, but she put her hands to my chest to stop me.

"I can't do this Aric," she said in a distant voice.

"Why not?" I asked her.

I knew she could feel how hard my dick was through my jeans. It was trying to break through the zipper as we spoke.

"I can't have sex with you again knowing you are married. It's not right."

"We can think about it not being right tomorrow," I told her as I caressed her round and posh rear again. "Right now all you need to think about is how good it's going to feel with me inside of you."

I gently lowered her face down to mine with one hand while the other hand found its way between her thighs. Her silky folds were so wet that my fingers felt like they were on a slip and slide. I moved her off of me and made quick work of dropping my jeans and boxers. I stroked my dick just for the hell of it, trying to stave off the aching need to be inside of her. Easing her back on top of me I slowly lowered her down onto my throbbing manhood. She moaned the sexiest moan and her head fell back. I almost lost it as my head fell back onto the base of the couch, biting down on my lip to keep from going crazy from being inside of her. I had to get myself together. Chyanne's pussy almost had me near tears. I don't even know how to explain what being inside of her felt like. Her soft folds were so hot, tight, and wet that all I could do was savor the feeling for a minute. As I listened to her breathing quicken, she was coming already and I hadn't even moved. Shit turned me on more. Made my dick jump.

"Damn baby, you miss me that much huh?" I teased her.

She was trying her best to hold it together so I gave her a little push to take her on over the edge. I slowly moved her up and down on me and that's all it took for her to rain down on me. I could feel her walls inhale and exhale as it gripped me. Her insides had a vice grip on me. I was about to lose myself inside of her until I saw the tears roll down her face.

"Please, don't make me do this, Aric. I can't. . . . you're married. It's not right . . ."

"Damn, Chyanne. Can't you worry about it not being right some other time?" I snapped, annoyed that she was playing with me.

She shook her head. As bad as I wanted to lay her on that couch and see if I could go for a world record and get her pregnant while she was already pregnant, I wouldn't be able to concentrate with her crying like I would be forcing myself on her. Been there, done that. I moved her off of me. Her insides even felt good when I was coming out of her. I stood, stepped completely out of my pants and walked to the bathroom in her bedroom so I could wash up, angry, displeased, and horny as ever! My dick was aching for a release and took me a while to get it to go down. After a while Gabe was calling me to tell me he was pulling into Chyanne's neighborhood. Chyanne was in her room with the door closed when I walked back into the front room to get dressed. After dressing, I walked into her room, kissed her forehead and told her I was leaving. She was lying down facing her window with her back to me. She didn't say anything.

Took me an hour to get home, could be because I was dreading having to hear Stephanie's mouth or could be because I was annoyed as hell with Chyanne. Either way when I got home, the house was quiet. Stephanie had Kenny G wafting low throughout the house. Even though this would be her first time officially sleeping in the house, she knew her way around it like she had been there before.

When I took the job in Atlanta, we were living in New York. I was working for Claxton Marketing and Advertising. I had wanted to get from under them for a while and the opportunity I was looking for came up sooner than I had realized. The guy that I'd worked directly under, Mark, gave me the inside information I needed to put my name into the hat to run B&G Marketing and Advertising. I didn't mind working for Claxton. I had been all over the world doing their dirty work, but I was the only brother on the twentieth floor and it looked as if that's where they wanted me to stay. I mean I was a top level executive, but I'd started wanting more of a challenge.

When Mark was chosen over me for VP of Marketing, I knew it was time for me to get the hell on. Mark was a hard worker, don't get me wrong, but that white boy couldn't find the floor if he fell on it. He took me along for the ride, but I got tired of doing all of the work and Mark getting the credit for it. He knew it and being the upstanding guy that he was he pulled some strings and got me the interview with B&G. After that, it was up to me to get the job. B&G wasn't as big as Claxton, but I was planning on changing all of that.

"Aric, is that you?" Stephanie called out to me.

"Who else would it be?" I answered as I took a beer from the fridge and popped the cap.

I took a huge swallow as I prepared to have to fight with Stephanie I knew was coming as soon as I heard her descend the stairs. I turned to look at her and it took me a minute to say anything. She was standing there naked as the day she came into the world. Her hair was pulled back into a ponytail, her perky breasts bounced as she moved around, and her pussy was bald. My dick started to throb again. Not so much because Stephanie turned me on, but because thoughts of being inside of Chyanne ran through me.

Stephanie walked over to me and took the beer from my hand, sitting it on the counter. I let her pull my shirt that was tucked inside of my jeans over my head. Standing on her tip toes she brought her lips to mine and rubbed my dick through my jeans. Our tongues played around with each other for a while before she dropped down and unzipped my pants after unbuttoning them. She snatched my pants down and that lower hanging part of me popped her in the eye for her affront. She giggled as she looked at me and stroked me slowly.

I didn't even know if my face held a reaction. All I could think about was that I had just left Chyanne and wondered if her scent was still on me even though I'd washed up. I tried to pull her up, but she stopped me and damn near swallowed me whole in one gulp. I had to grab a hold of the wall to keep my balance. Stephanie was an aggressive lover, always had been. So when she did anything you'd better be prepared for it. She was sucking my dick like her mouth had a vacuum suction.

"Good God . . ." I managed to moan out.

She gripped my shaft at the base and used her tongue in a swivel motion around my head almost causing my knees to go weak. She was deep throating me all the while using her tongue to tickle that sensitive part underneath my head. I quickly stepped out of my shoes and pants before I pulled her up and ushered her to the front room, bent her over the red sofa, and entered her from behind.

"Oh shit! Oh my God, Aric, you feel so good," she proclaimed.

I pulled her hair from the ponytail holder and grabbed a handful of it in my hand as it pooled around her face. As I pulled her hair, I pulled her back into me so her thrust could catch mine when she threw it back at me.

"Yes, baby, fuck me," she cried out again as her hand gripped the arm of the sofa.

I bent my knees and dipped under her so I could stroke her spot. Sweat started to form on my forehead as I worked her from behind. Although Stephanie's sex was good, my mind couldn't help but wonder back to how good it felt to be inside of Chyanne, even if only for a little while. As that thought crossed my mind, I pumped harder into Stephanie, letting her feel every inch of me and then some. Her walls locked around me as I could feel her working her muscles.

"This pussy will always be yours, baby, no matter what. Fuck me like you miss me, baby."

I let her hair go and gripped her around her waist. Her head fell forward and she let out my name loudly and declared that she was coming again. She arched her back, stood on her tip toes, and pushed back into me hard, swift, and vigorously.

"Come with me, baby," she crooned. "I want to feel you come in me. Go deeper, baby."

I obliged and dug deeper into her ocean. I could hear her juices splashing around in between us and I growled low in my throat. I felt my shaft swell and my head throb as I got ready to release all of my frustrations inside of her.

"That's right, baby, come with me . . . you feel so damn good, Aric! I miss this so much."

Once I felt like I was ready to explode, she moved, dropped to her knees, and allowed me to release inside of her mouth. It felt so good that my knees buckled. She sucked and sucked until I couldn't take anymore. Placing my hands on both sides of her head I removed her mouth and my breathing was out of control as my heart beat in my chest like it was trying to escape.

"You know that's my favorite," she said as she stood and smiled at me wiping her lips.

She went to kiss me on my lips and I turned my head. Her kiss landed on my jaw. She'd known not to try and kiss me after she did that.

She laughed before saying, "Hey, you might be surprised at how good you taste."

"I'll pass," I answered causing her to throw her head back in laughter again.

My first thoughts were food and I was about to ask her to make me something to eat.

"I'm going to go start the shower," she said preparing to leave the front room.

"Let me get something to drink and I'll be up right behind you."

"Okay, and don't take too long. I may have another surprise for you in the shower," she said as her giggle traveled up the stairs behind her.

I slowly walked back into the kitchen and grabbed a bottle of water from the fridge. The muscles in my legs throbbed and my mind traveled back to Chyanne. I couldn't help but to feel a little guilt that I'd had thoughts of her run through my mind while I'd had sex with Stephanie. Things were not always so cut and dry when it came to emotions and men, and I was one of those men who didn't really know what to do when he had too many at one time rolling around in his head. While I couldn't deny that I loved Stephanie, I could say that it was not as strong as it used to be.

I met Stephanie her first year in college. Gabe had always told me about his sister from Atlanta and that she was his father's child from his marriage. He'd been raised in Atlanta until his senior year when his dad had him and his mother move away. The way his dad told it, it was because he wanted Gabe to get into college up north. Let Gabe tell it, it was because his mom and Stephanie's mom wouldn't stop fighting. Stephanie's mom and Gabe's mom had been best friends until Gabe's mother slept with his father. Gabe and I had met when he had enrolled at Brooklyn Tech his senior year. We'd been boys every since. Gabe's father had called the night before Stephanie was to make it to New York and had asked me to help Gabe look out for her. Gabe and I were in our Sophmore year at NYU and I had no problem with doing what he'd asked.

I'd agreed, just because Gabe's dad had always been nice to me and he was there for me when my father was nowhere around. Meeting Stephanie for the first time was like looking at a goddess. Her dark skin, long wavy hair, hazel and green eyes, all called out to me. She was an exotic work of art and she was mine before we even left the airport. I knew that when she smiled at me and winked. Gabe and I quickly found out that she was not the angel of innocence that her father thought she was. By week four, she was sucking me off and I had already had sex with her by the end of week one. She didn't make too many female friends because she was catty and felt like no other woman was to be trusted. I'm sure what had happened between her mother and Gabe's mom had something to do with her way of thinking.

None of that mattered to me because, for the first time, I was in love. Stephanie and I were so wrapped up in each other that when my mom and her parents objected to us getting married, we ran off and did it anyway. We were married by the time she was twenty-three and I was twenty-four. You really couldn't tell us at the time that we weren't meant to be together. We were so into each other that nothing and nobody else mattered. Starting out, we had a really good marriage, and everything was decent at first. However, it quickly went downhill.

I couldn't even explain what happened. Nights of heated passion turned into days of cold calculated arguments. She was the first one to get a job in her field when she landed a job at a TV station as a producer. She quickly worked her way up the ladder becoming an executive producer in no time and I guess I didn't get the big-time corporate job fast enough for her. Even though I had graduated at the top of my class and had job offers, none of that was lucrative enough for her. Her father had old world money and she was used to getting what she wanted when she wanted. I guess what confused me about the whole thing was while we were in college and I was working a regular job, she didn't seem to mind. Once she graduated and got the job she wanted it was like to hell with me and my aspirations.

Stephanie had a way of making you feel like you weren't even good enough to breathe the same air as her. I can't say who started the cheating first, but we'd both done our share of it. I remember almost pushing her head through a wall when I had first found out she was cheating. My ego couldn't take the blow to my man hood. She'd been cheating with an old classmate of hers and just got sloppy enough to get caught. I won't lie to you and say that shit didn't hurt, because it tore me apart at the seams. I wanted to kill her I was so fucking pissed! She'd left her email open on the home computer and I just happened to want to print something before she could return from the bathroom. There it was in black and white, another man talking about how he enjoyed fucking my wife from behind.

At first, I thought it was some colossal joke. It had to be. *No way in hell Stephanie would be cheating on me* is what ran through my mind, but I just couldn't pull myself away from the words on that screen. She was telling him how she'd enjoyed the way he'd eaten her pussy and he in return told her how he'd enjoyed her dick sucking skills. Those were all their words and they were very explicit with one another. Before she could round the corner, I'd lost it and my hand was shoving her head into the nearest wall, knocking pictures down in the process.

After realizing that I'd been sitting at the computer she didn't even ask what was going on. When I snatched

her from the floor by the roots of her hair all she did
was stare at me with tears in her eyes. She didn't even
deny it, or offer an explanation as I yelled in her face
demanding some kind of clarification. That's when
she started her verbal assault, telling me that I wasn't
pleasing her the way I had been and yelling about me
caring more about my job than I did about her. Funny
thing was, I'd been working like a slave to make sure
she could have all of the things she was used to having.

Stephanie was a vicious woman and her words could
attack you and hurt worse than anything physical she
could throw at you. That was another thing, the physical altercations we'd had were enough to make anybody
think of divorce. The kind of marriage we had at the
moment was not what I had envisioned. Times changed
and so did people. She and I both had changed and it
didn't seem as if it was for the better, at least not when it
came to me and her.

I finished off the bottle of water and headed upstairs.
She was already out of the shower and drying off by the
time I had gotten in there.

"Took you too long so I just got out. I left the water
on for you," she said as she dried herself off.

"Took me a minute to get myself together. You took
the little strength I had away," I replied.

She smiled and looked away like she was thinking of
something.

"How did your meeting go with. . . . her?"

I knew it was coming sooner or later. "She got sick
and had to leave. Didn't really get much accomplished."

"What did you have to meet with her about anyway?"

I watched as she sat at the vanity mirror she'd bought
that same day and looked at me before grabbing her
mango body whip.

"Asked her for a DNA test on the baby," I answered.

She stop twisting the top, finally opening it and slowly laying it down, still keeping her eyes on me. "So, you don't think this baby is yours then?"

Before answering, I removed a wash cloth and bath towel from the linen closet. "I didn't say that. I have no doubt the baby is mine, just want to be sure for legal reasons."

She didn't hide the hurt on her face. At that moment, she stopped looking at me and started to apply the whip to her legs.

"So is she going to give you one?"

I removed my watch and wedding band before I answered her. "She's a high risk pregnancy and this could potentially hurt her and the baby. So she doesn't really want to give me one right now."

"You sure that's the only reason?"

"I'm positive."

She didn't say or ask anything else so I went ahead and showered. Thoughts of Chyanne still cluttered my mind. I needed to call and check on her before I closed my eyes for the rest of the night. Thoughts of the child she was carrying and the strong possibility that it could be mine brought a minute smile to my face. I still wanted to hold off on my excitement until I knew for sure.

Stepping out of the shower, I dried off, applied some baby oil to my skin and pulled on black cotton PJ's.

"I love you so much Aric and I really want this to work," she said to me after I had walked back into the bedroom. "There was so much passion in what we just did. I don't care what you have going on outside of these walls, I will always be where your heart is and you know that. You don't have to say anything back to me right now, but you know I'm telling the truth. We've been together for almost over twenty years and you know like I know nothing can compare to that."

There was silence between us after she said that. I had nothing to say. She felt one way about what had happened and I felt another. So to avoid hurting her feelings or another argument, I remained silent. I noticed my phone was lying on her vanity. I knew for a fact I'd left it downstairs. She saw where my vision had gone and decided to speak up.

"She called, wanted to speak with you. I told her we were busy and that she should not call this time of night unless it was an emergency."

I rolled my tongue over my teeth and licked my lips. I could feel my annoyance level rising.

"She's pregnant Stephanie. It could have been an emergency," I said as I folded my arms and turned to look at her.

She had her back resting against two pillows while sitting in the bed. "It wasn't. She said so."

She said that and cut her eyes at me like her word was final.

"Next time she calls, I would appreciate it if you let me handle her."

She only gave a tsk and slowly shook her head. "I don't want to fight Aric. Just come to bed. We can discuss her tomorrow."

"Nothing to discuss," I said as I turned the lights out.

"There is a lot we need to discuss just not tonight," she said as I crawled into bed.

My stomach growled and reminded me I was hungry.

"Why is your stomach growling? I thought you ate when you went out to meet her."

Anytime she said the word 'her' is was with spite. I was more concerned that we'd been together long enough for her to know that I was always hungry after sex. I reminded her of this and she laughed quietly.

"Well go and get something to eat. I'm tired and just want to fall asleep. I'll make it up to you tomorrow," she said before turning her back to me.

As sleepy as I was, hunger made me get up.

"Aric?"

"Yeah."

"Don't forget to clean up after you're done and pick your clothes up from the front room and the kitchen," she said.

"Go to sleep, Stephanie."

I couldn't help to think, as I made my way down the stairs, that Chyanne would have gotten up to cook for me and she would have picked up my clothes.

Chyanne

I was sitting in the lobby of the CheeseCake Factory waiting for Jamie to arrive. I had finally gotten back around to returning his phone calls. It took me a while because Aric and I had finally agreed that I would do the prenatal DNA testing. I knew I shouldn't have been agreeing to do it, but he wouldn't get off my back. It seemed that since I'd refused to have sex with him he had become more adamant about it, not letting up until I'd finally given in to his demands. I looked around the lobby glad to be feeling better after I'd started taking the Phenergan the doctor had prescribed for me. That helped so much with the nausea and dizziness that I'd been able to go out and get the things done that I'd been putting off, like grocery shopping.

I was sitting next to the bakery and the bar was behind me. I wished like hell I could have a drink but knew it was a no go. Sitting there I stared at the reflective glass in front of me and caught a glimpse of myself. I looked pretty decent. My hair was starting to get its fluff back. I hadn't straightened it since the first time Aric had talked me into it. I had dressed down in a nice pair of black dress slacks and a cotton mouth red dress shirt with red Chanel flats and a touch of chocolate MAC lip gloss was the only makeup I had on. Thoughts of the last conversation Aric and I had ran through my mind. He had come over the day before to make sure that I hadn't changed my mind about the testing. He was so cold and distant. He didn't try to come on to me like he usually did and I don't know why that bothered me. It shouldn't have, but it did, made me feel some type of way.

I hate to admit that I had wanted him to reach out and touch me, do something. I guess it had more to do with the fact that his wife had answered his phone and hung up on me when I called. That pissed me off, but I guess I'm glad she did that because it gave me clarity. I was about to ask him to come back and finish what he'd started a couple of nights before. My body had started to betray me. He didn't even sit down when I had offered him a seat. He just wanted to see that I had done the paperwork and that I had, indeed, talked to my doctor and made the appointment. My doctor was livid and insisted over and over that I think more about what I was doing and the risk it was putting on me and the baby. But I knew to get Aric off my back I would have to do it.

Looking at my watch, I pulled my sweater tighter when the front doors opened and a cool breeze wafted in. I really had a great disdain for the weather in Atlanta. One minute it was cold and the next it was hot, then the next it was raining and the humidity wreaked havoc on my hair. February was less than a couple of days away and the weather would only get worse from here on out until around late March, if even. I shivered and looked up into the face of Jamie.

He was as sexy as he had always been. His mocha colored skin and vibrant smile lit up the room while the neatly done locks spilled around his shoulders. His smile was instantly contagious and dark chocolate eyes reeled me in as well as a few of the other ladies in the room. His physique could be seen clearly from underneath his clothes. It was clear he was a man who took pride in his body and it wasn't lost on me that he caused most of the room to stop and stare. I quickly stood and went into his outstretched arms. Jamie had that kind of effect on me for some reason and I couldn't explain it. He made me as scatterbrained as a school girl.

"How are you?" he asked as he pulled me into a tight hug.

"I'm good," I responded.

"You smell nice. Look beautiful as well."

I giggled a bit as we both pulled away from the hug.

"Thank you," I said as I smiled up at him.

"How've you been?"

He asked me that after the hostess told us our wait would be another ten minutes. The Factory was pretty crowded for the lunch time rush. We had sat down on the bench I was occupying before he walked in.

"Pretty good, I suppose."

"You sure? I went to your job looking for you and they said you no longer worked there. I'd gotten worried when I didn't hear from you after your birthday."

I pretended to fix a button on my sweater to stave off the distressing feeling in the pit of my stomach before looking back into his inquiring gaze.

"Long story Jamie."

"Does it have anything to do with the bruises around your neck and on your face?"

Once again, I looked away from his piercing eyes. Jamie had always been able to look right through me. I could tell he was already drawing his own conclusions, but before I could give him an explanation the hostess came to escort us to our table. Once seated and after drinks had been ordered Jamie wasted no time getting back to the discussion at hand.

"Did Aric put his hands on you, Chyanne?"

I was kind of taken aback by the question and even more so by the tone of his voice. It was as lethal as the look in his eyes. I was too embarrassed to tell him the truth. Too afraid it would make him look at me differently.

"What? No. Why would you ask me that?" I lied and chuckled.

"So what happened?" he asked after he took a sip of his Long Island Iced Tea.

"His wife is what happened." I decided to tell him at least half of the truth.

Shock registered across his face and both his eyebrows arched.

"That dude is married?"

"Yes and before you assume I'm some home-wrecking whore, I didn't know."

He smirked and cast a skeptical look at me. It annoyed me.

"What the hell is that look for Jaime? I didn't know! I had no idea."

He shrugged. "Not saying that you knew he was married, but you had to know something."

I put my glass of water down on the table after taking a quick sip and stopped fumbling around with the napkin in my hand. I felt as if I needed to defend my character because it sure as hell felt as if it was being attacked.

He continued, "I mean when you were at my place over the New Years, you hinted that you had no idea what was going on with you two and whatever it was that you guys had. That tells me that you at least knew there was another woman or something."

I didn't say anything to that as tears started to sting my eyes. Had to be because of the hormones.

"I'm not saying any of this to make you feel bad Chyanne, but I have to be honest. The only time a man keeps a woman on a string like that is because there is another woman. You had to know something. The signs had to be there. So whether you knew he had a wife or not, you knew there was another woman."

I still didn't say anything. What could you say when you had just been read like a book? Jamie didn't look as if it had bothered him to do it either.

I wiped the tears from my eyes and asked, "So you think I'm stupid, huh?"

He leaned forward and clenched his hands together. "Nah. I think you're a smart young woman who made a stupid decision. We've all been there Chyanne."

"Gee, thanks!"

"Hey, I wouldn't be your friend if I couldn't be honest with you," he said sitting back and taking another swallow of his drink.

We sat silent for another minute or so as our waitress set out appetizers on the table. We had both decided to share Sweet Corn Tamale Cakes.

After we both took a few bites, he wiped his mouth and asked, "So his wife just out of the blue attacked you?"

I briefly told him the whole story of what had happened the day Aric's wife attacked me. I knew he was getting a kick out of the animated way I was moving my hands telling him the story. He actually laughed out loud when I told him the reason I fought back was because the slap hurt so badly that I couldn't think straight. My only reaction was to reach out and grab the first person within snatching distance!

"At that moment, I was so sick of people putting their hands in my face. I've been getting slapped since

I was a kid. My dad slapped me so many times I lost count. So when Aric slapped me the night before and then this unknown woman . . . ."

I stopped talking when his facial expression hardened and his eyes darkened. He slowly sat his drink back down on the table and balled his lips.

"What?" I asked.

He grimaced before speaking. "You just said Aric put his hands on you. When I asked you earlier, you said no."

I sat back in my chair when I realized my mistake. Swallowing hard, I looked away from him and dropped my hands to my lap.

"How many times has he hit you Chyanne?"

"Look, Jamie it's not like you're thinking. We were arguing. Tempers were flaring. I hit him, he hit me—"

"That's no damn excuse for the man to be putting his hands on you! Don't be stupid Chyanne."

His voice was laced with so much venom that my defenses immediately shot up and April came to mind. He sounded so much like her when she was being condescending. I was sick of people calling me stupid too. Hell, Aric and I wouldn't have even been arguing if Jamie wouldn't have come to my job and kissed me in front of everybody. or even if he wouldn't have sent those pictures to me!

I tried to tell him as much. "We were only arguing because you decided to show up—"

"Oh, so it's my fault he's whooping your ass?"

He'd said that so loudly that I quickly dropped my head when people at surrounding tables started to look at us.

I leaned forward and said through clenched teeth. "He's not beating me. He slapped me once."

"Once is too many damn times and I'm willing to bet it's been more than once."

I don't know, but it was something in his voice, his eyes. The way he was looking at me made me feel as if he was calling me all kinds of dim-witted fools in his mind. He had one arm on the table and one on his lap. His jaw was twitching and he was looking at me directly in my eyes each time I got enough nerve to look across the table at him. He made me feel stupid.

"Screw you, Jamie. I didn't come here for you to judge me," I came back with, and threw the napkin that had been in my lap on the table.

I stood and was preparing to leave him sitting at the table alone when he stood and gently placed his hand around my wrist to stop me.

"Please, Chyanne. Sit down. I'm sorry."

We stood that way staring at each other until I noticed other people starting to gawk at us so I sat down first. The waitress appeared as soon as we had sat down and I could tell by the look on her face that she had been waiting to see if she should bring the food over. We sat quietly as she set our food out in front of us and Jaime stared at me. I knew by the way he was looking at me that he was trying to assess which bruises were from Aric and which came from the fight between me and his wife.

After the waitress left he said to me, "I didn't mean to offend you, Chy, but the truth is someone needs to tell you what you don't want to hear and I love you enough to do that."

By now tears were raining down my face because I knew he was right on so many levels. Aric had abused me on more than one occasion, but I was too embarrassed to admit it, especially to Jaime. I wiped my eyes and tried to pull myself together.

"Has he hit you more than once, Chyanne?"

"Hit? No."

I could see one of Jaime's legs shaking as we both sat there and looked at one another. It was a tense moment for the both of us, more so for me. I didn't know what Jaime thought of me at that moment but, I could tell his mood had changed. He had folded one arm under the other while his right hand covered his mouth like he was trying to keep what he was going to say in.

"Abuse is abuse, no matter what form Chyanne," he said as he leaned forward with both elbows on the table.

"Can we please not talk about this anymore Jamie?"

"Talk about what? The fact that he and his wife are whooping your ass? What part of the game is that baby?"

I rubbed my hand across my forehead to try and stave off the headaches I felt coming on. "Please Jaime. Not now."

"If not now then when. You have to face the facts sooner or later."

"I will and I am. Just. . . . can we talk about this later and somewhere else?"

This time I looked at him dead on hoping that it would help me to get him to stop talking about it. He stared at me for a couple of seconds before deciding to let it go. We ate in silence for a while after that, both of us picking at the food we had ordered because it was clear that the mood had changed and our appetites had gone. I figured since Jamie probably already thought I was a stupid home wrecking whore, I might as well have finished telling him everything.

"I'm pregnant," I whimpered out.

I looked over at Jamie and his fork had stopped an inch away from his lips.

"I'm sorry, what?" he asked.

I exhaled and laid my fork down. "I said I'm pregnant Jamie."

He sat all the way back in his chair, wiped his mouth, and dropped his white cloth napkin on the table. "Wow. Wasn't expecting that."

"Yeah, neither was I."

I could tell by the way he'd slowly rubbed the back of his neck and the way his eyes had widened that he was indeed as shocked as I was when I found out I was pregnant.

"Wow," he exclaimed again before asking, "Who's the father?"

"What?"

"The father, who is he?"

"Aric."

"Are you sure?"

"Yes, Jamie, I'm sure. But to calm the questions I know you're about to ask, I'm going to have a prenatal DNA test just to be one hundred percent sure. You and Aric are the only men I've ever had sex with, so if he isn't the father, you are. And I doubt that because the doctor said I was twelve to thirteen weeks pregnant and you and I only had sex two or three weeks ago. So there."

I said all of that, put it all out there so he could stop asking me questions and stop looking at me like he was disgusted that I was even in his presence. As I looked over at him I couldn't tell what he was thinking and after he only stared at me with a look that I couldn't read, I decided it was time for me to go.

"Will you excuse me?" he asked me. "I need to go to the restroom. Don't leave. I'll be back."

I would have done just what he'd asked me not to do if he hadn't kissed my cheek on his way to the restroom. I don't know why he did it but it put me at ease.

I shook my head and chuckled at myself. I had done some really silly mess in the last couple of months. More stuff than I'd done in my entire life. I'd had sex with two men in less than six months and one of them was married. I shook my head thinking, if my mother could see me now, what would she think? I always heard her ranting about how only whores slept around with married men and the dumb ones did and claimed they didn't know about it. My mom may not have made the best decision when she chose to stay with my dad and she may have sometimes looked the other way when he used his hand to get his point across, but anytime he put his hands on me all hell broke loose. Maybe that's why although at times I really disliked her for staying with my father, there were other times when I thought about the harsher beatings she would take for defending me.

I was about to signal the waitress for the check when I looked up and into the face of the woman who had attacked me days before. Aric's wife was walking right toward me. Now out of all the places in Atlanta to eat, why did we both have to choose the same location? I was hoping she was looking past me and would keep walking, but no such luck.

She was a very pretty woman. Her beauty was almost intimidating and made me wonder what man in his right mind would cheat on her? She was a slim sister with a nice a breast-to-waist, hip-to-ass ratio. Her skin was flawless, dark and very exotic looking, even with the slight bruises and scratches that I could still make out on her face. The red knee-length dress she had on hugged all of her curves in the right places causing men to gape shamelessly, and the CL heels she had on only accentuated it.

I could tell by the look on her face that she had spotted me and that she had something she wanted to say. At that moment, I made up in my mind that if she chose to sit down and talk to me, I would tell her whatever she wanted to know. I could be a woman and admit that I had slept with her husband, but she needed to know that not one time did Aric tell me he was married. She needed to know that I was not the woman she saw me as, but as soon as she stopped at my table and folded her arms with a nasty sneer planted across her face I knew it would not go the way I was hoping.

"So we meet again," she stated.

I didn't respond just yet. I needed to know what her motive was for approaching me first.

"I know you're not playing shy, Chyanne! You weren't too shy to be fucking my husband," she all but yelled.

People around us started to stare again. It seemed as if I put on a show no matter where I was or who I was with.

"Why don't you have a seat so we can talk like adults—"

She laughed at my candor. "Adults? Talk? What do we have to talk about? I just wanted to see the fat bitch that thought she could screw my husband and get away with it."

"Look, I didn't even know—"

"Don't even try me with that, 'I didn't know he was married' crap. There were plenty of times that we were on the phone together and I could hear you in the background asking who I was. I know it was you because you have that same squeaky ass voice and I know my husband; he would have told you about me, if you would have asked."

She was annoying the hell out of me and I was surprised by my own anger. It wasn't like me to encourage any type of confrontation, but she was pushing my buttons.

"I told you, I didn't know he was married. If you know him so well, then why didn't he tell me he had a wife? Not one time did he mention you," I snapped.

"To not know he was married means you are not only a slut, but a stupid one! I don't know what you think is going to happen, or what you want to happen, but it's over. Aric doesn't want you. I'm Mrs. McHale and I will always be!"

Why was it that every woman that fixed her mouth to call me stupid turned out to be the stupid one? She's the one who had no idea her husband was cheating on her, but I was the stupid one? I was in his house, the house that I am sure she was at with him and there was not one article of anything there that even remotely resembled him having a wife. I was not about to sit there and allow her to get me any more worked up than I already was.

"Okay, it's obvious that Aric has lied to the both of us. So it's not either one of our faults that we find ourselves here, but he's the one you need to be talking to, not me."

"I've talked to my husband. Trust me on that, but now I want to talk to the little girl who's gone and gotten herself pregnant by my husband. Baby or no baby, he will never leave me. You were just one of the many women he slept with. No matter how many times he's done it, he always comes back to me, back home! You were just a piece of pussy and from what I'm hearing an easy piece of pussy at that. Stop calling my husband. Leave him alone. And, let me tell you, your arms aren't long enough to box with me. Try me, and I will take that little bastard you're pregnant with. Me and my husband will be raising the baby you carry. My arms reach a long way, Chyanne. I'm not the one you want to go to battle with."

Now she had gone too far. Her making a threat to my child was more than I was willing to take. If I wasn't afraid of getting arrested, I would have dropped her where she stood. My eyes started to water I wanted to lay hands on her so badly. From that second she had crossed the line. I had no clue as to what Aric had been telling her, but she'd started barking up the wrong tree. I stood so I could prepare to leave. The waitress had placed the check on the table and quickly disappeared. I felt as if everybody was watching the scene unfolding, waiting to see what would happen next. I quickly looked around to see if I could spot Jaime and caught the glances of people who were watching me. Some looked as if they were just waiting for the fists to fly, while others looked at me with derision. Of course, I was the bad guy.

"No, you sit," she said as she pushed me back down in the chair. "I'm not done talking to you yet.

I was too in shock to react right away, more so because I fell back hard and I felt a jolt in my stomach. My hands quickly went to my stomach. As I was about to jump back up and lay her out, Jamie's hand on my shoulder stopped me. I was shocked when Stephanie tried to slap me and Jaime pushed her back.

"Back up and leave her alone," he said to her as he stood in front of me.

Stephanie stumbled and almost fell back but caught herself. I could tell she was appalled by him pushing her and had hurt her ankle trying to break her fall.

"Come on, Chyanne. Let me take care of the check so we can get out of here. You okay?" he asked.

I nodded and stood when he pulled my chair out. We both stopped and looked when Stephanie moved around him so she could see me. Jamie kept himself planted firmly between the both of us so she had to move at an angle to see me. It was clear that people were trying to gather whether if Jamie was the husband in question or not.

"Stay away from my husband. I won't say it again," she pointedly told me as she made her way to the lobby with a slight limp.

Jamie shook his head and after paying the check we both walked out. We were both quiet as he walked me to my car. I didn't know what he was thinking of me, but I couldn't really think about that at the moment. He wrapped his arms around me when I tried to run away from the wind blowing at me. He smelled so good and he was warm.

So many things were running through my mind like, *What had Aric told that woman about me for her to act that way?* I mean, I knew she was upset about him cheating on her, but some of the things she said stuck out to me. Like, how many times he had cheated on her. I knew it was dumb, but it hurt to hear that. I didn't know why I felt jealous in that moment.

"You want to talk about it?" Jamie asked when we had reached my car.

I unlocked the door, got in, and started the engine before turning back to answer him.

"I wouldn't even know where to start."

He squatted and placed his hand on my leg. "What the hell happened in there? All I kept hearing was people talking about some woman confronting another about her husband and I knew it had to be you."

I glanced at him quick and hard when he said that.

"I didn't mean it like you think Chyanne. I meant that . . . never mind. Tell me what happened."

"I really would rather not rehash it right now. Can I call you later and we can talk?"

He nodded and placed a gentle kiss to my lips before standing. I wanted to ask him why he did things like that, but my phone started to ring. I knew it was Aric because of the ring tone.

"Call me when you get in and let me know that you've made it home safely. I have to go down to Ellenwood and check on a few things at one of my stores so maybe I can stop by later and we can do a movie or something. Cool?"

I smiled. "Cool. Call you later," I said to him as he closed my door for me.

I had pulled out of the parking spot and was about to pull out into traffic when I remembered my manners. I turned to see Jamie walking to where I assumed his car was parked. I didn't know why I didn't ask if he would have liked me to drive him to his car. I looked for a way to get out into traffic so I could pull along-side him and ask just that. By the time I had made the u-turn he had stopped and was talking to some woman who looked so much like Jill Scott it was uncanny. Don't ask me why my face frowned and I looked like I had been slapped. They were both smiling at one another and when they exchanged business cards my jealousy meter shot through the roof. I finally pulled up and let the window down.

"Sorry I didn't ask before, but would you like me to drive you to your car?" I asked him.

He excused himself and briskly walked over to the passenger side window before squatting and looking at me.

"No, I'm good. Why don't you go ahead and get home so you can get out of this traffic."

I looked past his shoulders at the Jill Scott look-a-like and looked back at him. He gave a slight chuckle and smirk.

"Please, don't tell me I see what I think I see."

"And, what's that?" I asked clearly defensive.

"Are you jealous, Chyanne?"

"No! I was just wanting to make sure you were okay is all," I lied.

He knew I was lying but was mature enough to laugh it off. "Go home Chyanne. I will call you later."

I shook my head at myself as I drove off. I had too much going on to be jealous over a woman talking to Jaime. I couldn't believe I'd even gone there. Aric was calling me again and it quickly brought me back to the reality of my situation.

Aric

I knew something was wrong as soon as she answered the phone. Her voice was low and even. Anytime Chyanne was mad, I could tell by that low and even tone her voice carried. My first guess was that she was still mad about having to do the prenatal DNA test. She had been acting that way since she had signed the papers and made the appointment for it. I guess what she didn't understand was that I needed her to do it for my sanity. She may have thought it was selfish on my part, but as a man I needed to know for a fact if I was bringing a child into the world. It was what it was and I wouldn't make any apologies for it.

"Why do you sound like that? What's wrong with you?" I asked after I had excused myself from the lunch my bosses and I were having.

She was quiet a minute before answering. I could hear her radio and the noise from traffic in her background.

"I saw your wife today," was all she said.

I sighed loud enough for her to hear me. That was enough for me to know all I needed to know, but I asked her about it anyway as I made a mental note to call Stephanie.

"And that's why you're upset?"

"No. I'm upset because she put her hands on me again and I'm upset because . . ."

She stopped talking like she had lost her train of thought or as if she changed her mind about saying what it is she had wanted to say. I took a seat on the bench across from the room the meeting was being held in. Although the board had agreed to look the other way about the incident my wife had caused when she attacked Chyanne, I was not about to take any chances with them finding out that I had really been sleeping with my executive assistant. I was careful in my conversation with her because people were still talking around the office and the last thing I needed was for the board to hear anything. I assured them that what had happened with Stephanie would never happen again. Yeah, I had to throw a little lie here and there when it came to me and Chyanne, but what had to be done, had to be done.

"Because what? What happened between you two that has you all bent out of shape?"

I could hear her breathing, sounded as if she was crying. "She put her hands on me and she threatened my child. She threatened to take my child away from me."

My brows creased. "What?"

She made a sniffling sound that let me know for sure she was crying. "She threatened to take my baby away from me, Aric!" She said in a shrill causing her voice to rise an octave.

"Chyanne, relax. Where are you right now?"

"On my way home," she said.

Her voice had relaxed a bit, but I could tell she was still rattled. I had no idea what the hell Stephanie had said to her, but the last thing I needed was for Chyanne to be stressed the day before the testing was to be done.

"I'll stop by and check on you later when I get off. You just relax and don't let Stephanie get to you. You have nothing to worry about. Just go home, relax, and wait for me, okay? We'll talk when I get there."

After she reluctantly agreed, I hung up and called Stephanie. She didn't answer. She probably already knew why I was calling and was preparing her side of the story. One thing was for certain, if the baby was mine she sure as hell would have to get used to Chyanne being around. As far as her taking the baby, she could hang that shit up. I would put my foot in her ass before I allowed that to happen.

I walked back into the room and took my seat. All of the members of the board were in a happy mood. Gabe and I had just gotten a merger deal on the table between B&G Marketing and Charter Marketing Team. If we played our cards right, we would be the biggest market-ing and advertising firm in the region in no time. We had been at lunch for about two hours and I was ready to get back to the meeting so I could call it a semi-early day. I was tired as hell and what Chyanne had told me about Stephanie had my nerves on end.

I cleared my throat to get everyone's attention. "If you guys don't mind, I would like to wrap up these final slides so we can all get out of here and call it a day. We've been here since six this morning and I don't know about you, but I could use the rest of the day off. So, let's get started."

I waited a few minutes for everyone to discard their trash and to get resituated before I continued. While they did that I put the Power Point presentation back up on the screen.

"As we all know an average company loses anywhere between ten and thirty percent of their customers a year. What we hope to do with this merger is to cut those numbers in half for the company contracts we've acquired."

"What's the time frame on that McHale?"

That was Davies Devereaux. The one man on the board that seemed to get a kick out of countering anything I put on the table. He was a good ole boy. The kind that you knew called you a "nigger" as soon as you turned your back. I made an attempt to smile and continued on.

"If we can get the companies to not only upgrade some of their technologies, but also to change the way their people work, we can take a company like Henderson MotorSports and turn them around in less than two years max."

He sat straight up and leaned forward. If I could take my truck and run him over I would. He was a blond-haired blue-eyed red neck and he seemed to think that no matter what I had done to turn the company around, I still wasn't fit to run it.

"A company like Henderson MotorSports you think would be a good risk for this company to continue to take on? I mean we will have to cut clients and we may as well start with a company that doesn't seem to take our hard work to heart, wouldn't you agree McHale?" He asked.

"On paper Henderson MotorSports may look like a disaster, but this is a huge company and they are cleaning house. So the way Aric and I see it is if we get our hooks into the CEO and run these numbers by him, he would have no choice but to agree to do what we say if he wants his company to stay afloat. A good customer service strategy should balance costs, quality, and revenues." Gabe started to speak up and leaned forward on the table so he could look Davies dead on. He didn't like Davies any more than I did.

"And with Henderson the quality isn't the problem," I continued. "We would need to get the costs down and the revenue up. We could do that in no time and get this company back on the road to recovery. We all know that a good thorough clean throughout the company can work miracles," I joked.

While half of the room laughed and the other smiled and agreed, Devereaux only eyeballed me and Gabe. I knew it fucked up his day to see two "boys" running his father's company, but by the time Gabe and I took this company above and beyond, we would have enough clout to shut him up. Gabe and I wrapped the meeting up. After all of the handshaking and bullshit talk, I was ready to go. Gabe and I waited until they were all gone before we celebrated.

"Man, this is huge," Gabe laughed as we gave each other handshakes and pats on the back.

"Damn, man. I can't believe we just pulled that off. Huge fucking deal we just came through with," I said to him.

"Right, even though Davies Devereaux seems to have it in for you. What did you do to that man to make him hate you the way he does?"

"Hell if I know. Knowing the racist bastard, he probably can't take me running this company and you know he's shitting bricks now that we've made this merger and you're on board now too."

Gabe took a seat on the couch in my office while I grabbed the Patron Platinum and poured us each a shot. He'd been a part of Charter since graduating college and had been all around the globe working a different office each year as the head of their marketing team. Luckily we both ended up in the same area at the same time and had put together a plan to merge that neither company could turn down, especially not with all the money that stood to be made.

"In the mouth and over the tongue, look out stomach here it comes," Gabe said.

I downed my drink and chuckled. His father used to say that all the time and he was the person to give me my first shot of alcohol. As I was about to ask Gabe how the old man was doing, my new assistant walked in. The one thing that I hated was a pretty woman who was dumber than a bag of rocks. Days like today were when I missed Chyanne. Cassie was a beautiful young woman but she didn't know her left from her right. If I didn't hire another assistant soon, she was going to drive me crazy.

"Mr. McHale, I'm sorry, but I can't find the file you're asking for," she whined.

Another thing that annoyed me was a whining ass woman. I simply looked at her as I sat on the corner of my desk. It was clear that I was making her uncomfortable with my silent staring. Basically she was just decoration because she wasn't worth the money I was paying her. She stood there in a red thigh length skirt suit that hugged the minimal curves she had. Her naturally curly hair fell to her shoulders and her dark brown eyes watered. With her skin turning red she slowly turned, looked at Gabe quickly before walking out of my office. I watched as she plopped down in her desk and started to look for the file again.

Gabe chuckled, "You're a mean old bastard. You could have at least told her where to look. Did you make her cry?" He asked as he turned to look at her and chuckled again. "Bet you're missing Chyanne now, huh?"

"It makes no damn sense for her to be that pretty and be as dumb as she is. That's a waste of woman. She's only good for fucking."

Gabe's eyes widened. "You—"

"No. Just making an observation is all," I said as I stood. "I'll get with you later on tonight though after I go and see Chyanne."

He stood and asked, "How is she? How's the pregnancy treating her?"

"Pregnancy is going good as far as I know. She was bitching about Stephanie threatening her earlier."

"Say what?"

"Yeah."

"I knew that was coming though. You know how Stephanie is when she's mad," he said and I nodded my head in agreement with him. "When did this happen?"

"Apparently within the last couple of hours. When I excused myself from the room it was her on the phone. Said something about Stephanie threatening to take the baby."

I gathered my lap top and brief case so I could get out of that office. It was starting to annoy me, especially talking about Stephanie and her scare tactics.

"Whoaaa! That's not cool," he said as we made our way out of my office.

I looked at Cassie. "Don't leave until that file is on my desk," I said to her.

She looked as if her feelings were hurt. "Yes sir," she mumbled.

Gabe and I made small talk as we rode the elevator down to the parking deck. We talked a little more about the merger, the excitement of it all and talked about how we would be rearranging the offices. It was more than likely that we would have to upgrade to a new office space. We made plans to meet up later for more celebratory drinks and I made my way home.

I'd been asleep for all of two hours when I heard Stephanie come barging up the stairs. I kept my eyes closed after glancing at the digital clock on the night stand by the bed in hopes that she wouldn't try to talk to me. I hadn't meant to come home and fall asleep, but after I'd worked out, showered, and eaten, the bed called to me. I watched as she deliberately made as much noise as she could. She slammed her clutch purse on the dresser and kicked her shoes across the room. Over the last couple of days boxes of her personal items had arrived and my house was no longer looking like the bachelor's pad I had set it up to be.

"Can't believe that son of bitch put his hands on me," I heard her mumble as she snatched her bracelets and watch off.

That caught my attention and made me wonder who the hell she was talking about. My phone vibrated on the dresser and I watched as she looked to see if I was still sleeping before she picked it up. She had a noticeable limp and I had to wonder if Chyanne had whooped her behind again.

"Hello," she answered.

I knew it was Chyanne. My phone only vibrated when she called.

"He's not here. What do you want with my husband?"

Stephanie was rocking from side to side with one hand on her hip. "I said he isn't here—"

I guess Chyanne must have hung up on her since she pulled the phone away from her ear and looked it like it had offended her. She slammed my phone down on the dresser and disappeared into the bathroom. As much as I just wanted to lay there and sleep, I knew that I needed to get up and go to see Chyanne like I'd said I would. I threw the covers from my body and slowly sat up on the side of the bed. Listening to Stephanie throw things around in the bedroom and mumble to herself made me want to get out of the house quicker. I knew

Stephanie and I knew it would only take a second for her to turn her anger on me. One thing that I was done with was fighting with her. I had come to that conclusion a long time ago. I often wondered if that was the reason I was so attracted to Chyanne. Chyanne was peace. She calmed me when was I was upset. One look at her sometimes and everything seemed right in the world.

"Where're you going?" Stephanie asked abruptly when she came out and saw me getting dressed.

"Going to talk to Chyanne."

I pulled on my boxer briefs and a pair of sweats before pulling on a thick white T-shirt.

"What are you going to talk to her for?"

I didn't answer her until I walked out of the closet and had stepped into my shoes. "She's having the DNA test tomorrow."

Standing as she talked with her hands, she shrugged. "So what does that have to do with you going to see her tonight?"

She was quickly annoying me. The attitude in her voice was like nails on a chalk board.

"So when do we talk about our marriage and what we're going to do about it?" She asked as she followed me to the bathroom, leaning against the post of the door as I washed my face.

In that moment, I felt as if we didn't do something about it soon, our living arrangement was only going to get worse. I had asked her to stay in New York when I moved down to Atlanta because I felt as if there was nothing left of our marriage to fix. I had washed my hands of the whole thing, but as time moved on and nostalgia set in, I had begun to miss her in a sense, or miss her familiarity. So, I started to accept her phone calls and I was surprised when we started having civilized conversations. Did that stop me from wanting Chyanne? No.

"What did you do to Chyanne today?" I asked, more so to let her know that I knew what she'd done and to get her to change the subject.

"What do you mean what did I do to her?"

We both had stopped what we were doing and were now looking at one another.

"Did you put your hands on her? Threaten to take her baby?"

I gave her a look that told her I wasn't in the mood for her bullshit. She huffed and gave a faux chuckle before looking at me as if I had grown horns out of my head.

"Excuse me? Are you really asking me about . . ." She chuckled again and stopped talking with a dramatic flair before continuing. "I don't get you! I don't understand you, Aric! What is it about this one that has you so up in arms?"

"What the hell does any of that have to do with you threatening my child or putting your hands on Chyanne for that matter?"

"I didn't threaten . . . that baby and all I did was push her down in the chair she had been sitting in—"

"While she is carrying my baby, you keep your damn hands to yourself!"

The look she gave me was murderous. It's like my words had slapped her and she wanted to return the favor.

"You better make sure it's your baby," she almost too calmly replied as I snatched my phone, keys, and wallet and placed them in the pocket of the sweats I had on.

I ignored her as I walked back into the bathroom and began brushing my teeth.

"I'm just saying Aric," she continued. "After all I'm sure the guy she was eating lunch with probably thinks it's his baby too with the way he was defending her."

She smirked when I stopped brushing my teeth long enough to spit and look at her. I finished up while she stood there and watched me. After a while her smirk turned into a full sneer. I finished and moved past her to make my way down the stairs. She followed at a slow pace. By the time I had gotten two bottles of water from the fridge and had grabbed an apple she was standing at the island in the kitchen with her hip pressed against it. I'd learned over the years that Stephanie was like a viper. As long as you didn't stare at it head on and get right in its face, it wouldn't strike; as long as I ignored her, she wouldn't keep talking. She hated to be ignored or told no.

"What is it about her, Aric? What is it about her that makes you disrespect your home the way you do or the woman that's been with you through everything?" She asked after she saw I was making my way to the door and I wasn't about to argue with her. "Answer me Aric! Don't ignore me!"

She was like a spoiled ass child and I wasn't in the mood to cater to her temper tantrum. Besides, my mind was on who the hell Chyanne was at lunch with. I had a good idea being that she claimed to have slept with only one other man.

"Aric!"

Stephanie yelled at me and pulled me from my thoughts. I looked at her . . . hard. Hoping that what I was feeling showed on my face. I really wanted her to leave me alone at that moment. Moving my keys around mindlessly in my pocket I was about at ready to punch something and she was getting on my damned nerves.

"What? What? What do you want? Why the fuck do you keep calling me? What do you want?" I had snapped that before I realized what I had done.

"Don't yell at me because you're mad that your bitch was with another man. Don't take that out on me," she said using velar pronunciations and dramatics to point at me then back to her chest.

I threw a bottle of water against the wall out of anger. I didn't even know why I was angry or maybe I did. Maybe I was angry because Chyanne was out with another man. Maybe I was angry at the thought of her being with someone else. Maybe I was angry that the longer I stood there and listened to Stephanie bitch, the longer Chyanne could have been letting another motherfucker get what I wanted so badly. I hadn't been able to get inside of her like I'd wanted to for too damn long and I wanted that shit badly. The thought of Chyanne letting somebody else between her thighs had me overheated.

Stephanie chuckled and shook her head as she looked at the water slowly drizzling down the wall. "Is it like that now? You want to get to her that bad?" She asked and gave a fake chuckle again. "Do you even care how I feel about this whole thing? To know that my husband is the father of a baby that doesn't belong to us?" Tears fell down her face as she spoke.

"If I said I cared would that make you feel better? If I said I was sorry would that make you feel better? Because I don't care and I'm not sorry. You didn't want to give me a baby. You're the one who started this whole 'I want a divorce' thing. So now, I found someone to give me what I want."

"So you planned this?" Her eyes squinted and she looked as if I repulsed her.

"No, I didn't plan it, but what's done is done. I can't take that shit back. Chyanne is having my baby whether you like it or not and you will not put your hands on her again as long as she's carrying my seed. I won't say that shit again."

She got in my face. "And what if I do Aric? What are you going to do? Whoop my ass?"

"Get out of my face Stephanie," I told her as I pushed her off of me and backed away from her.

She knocked my hand away from her. "She really has some hold on you huh? What is it about this young ass girl that you can't shake? You claim not to love her," she yelled as she continued, "yet she's special enough to make you treat me like I aint shit to you no more! You know how that makes me feel?"

Once again I had to push her out of my face. She fell and hit the floor hard, her hands flailing around wildly as she tried to grab a hold of the bar to break her fall. I hadn't meant to use that much force, but before I could try to apologize she was up. I knew what would happen next so I was prepared when she tried to slap me.

I grabbed both her wrists and shook her. "What is wrong with you?" I yelled at her. "Learn to keep your damn hands to yourself." Her hair shook wildly around her face as she twisted and turned trying to get out of my grip. "Damn. Why do you always have to make me put my hands on you in order for you to get it? Keep your damn hands to yourself."

"Fuck you Aric for taking us through this. You had to get that bitch pregnant," she kicked, yelled, and screamed like a mad woman as tears fell down her face like rapid raindrops. "I hate you for this! I would have given you another baby," she cried. "You didn't have to do this . . ."

I bent my head to look at her as I spoke. "Given me another baby? You already had your chance. That last life you took from me was the last chance you had. You want to make this out to be as simple as you giving me another child and you know as well as I do that there is more to it than that." My tone was harsh, but for the life of me I needed her to understand that our time together had passed.

"But I love you Aric . . ."

"Sometimes love isn't enough. If you loving me all of these years has caused as much pain as we brought each other then I don't want it."

"I'm ready now. The games, the lies, the hurt, the deceit . . . it's all done baby. I swear," she cried with a begging tone in her voice.

"I hear you. I hear what you're saying, but it's not enough! I'm all burned out!"

She screamed at me. Used her knee to try and hurt me in the area that was aching to be inside of another woman just minutes before. She was hurting and I knew that, but staying together wouldn't make me feel any better and it definitely wouldn't make her happy. I kept my hold on her until she stopped moving and calmed down enough to lay her forehead on my chest. She cried silently as we both stood there. It was clear that we were no longer good for one another. I had no idea why she was trying to fight to hold on to something that had nothing left.

In that moment I realized over and over again why I had agreed to give her a divorce the last time she'd asked for one. I don't know her reasons for wanting one at the time, but I was at the point where I was tired of her throwing the possibility of a divorce in my face. I was just tired of her period! I would always have love for Stephanie, but we could no longer stay married to one another and remain sane. It was obvious. I finally let her wrists go and tried to move her away from me so I could leave.

She grabbed my shirt as she looked up at me. "Are you still having sex with her?"

"What?"

"Are you still having sex with her? Did you have sex with her the same night we had sex?"

Immediately my heart rate picked up. I didn't fathom she would ask that question. The fact that I'd come so close to having sex with Chyanne the same night that I had sex with her did cause me some kind of self-reproach. She was staring intently at me, searching my face for the truth before my mouth could tell her. I could have gone into detail about what happened, but that would start another fight. A fight I didn't feel like fighting. I forced her hands out of the fisted clench she had on my shirt. She let out a sound similar to a person taking their last breath.

"Oh . . . my God! You did, didn't you?" she asked as I took my keys from my pockets. "You fucked her and then came here to let me suck your dick afterwards. You let me suck her pussy off of you. You dirty son of a bitch."

I didn't say anything as I continued to make my way to the door with her verbal insults being hurled at my back. As I cracked the door, I heard what sounded like a wounded cat and the next thing I felt was her nails in my neck as one of her open handed slaps beat me in the back of the head. I ducked my head at the onslaught of her attack and wrapped my mind around the fact that she was, once again, physically attacking me. I slammed the door so hard and fast the glass threatened to break.

When I turned to face her I'm sure my face held silent, deadly rage. I could tell because of the way her eyes widened and she stumbled back trying to get away from me. I don't know what ire my face held but it was enough to make her scream as I reached out and grabbed her throat. Before I could stop myself, her feet had left the floor, and she went flying against the wall. I'd thrown her so hard that she fell with enough force to knock the wind out of her. All I saw was a blurred vision of her face and blotches of red as she tried to make a swift movement away from me.

"I'm sorry Aric," she yelled as she swung her fists wildly and used her feet as a defense mechanism to get away from me.

I snatched her legs to bring her back to me, used her throat to pick her up from the floor, and slammed her against the wall again. Only this time, I didn't release her. The tip of her toes scraped the floor and her eyes watered as her nails dug into my hands and wrist. After that defense didn't work, she went for my face. She slapped, punched, and tried to scratch her way out of the hold I had on her neck.

I slammed her head into the wall. "How many times have I asked you to stop putting your hands on me?" I asked as I yelled in her face. Spittle from my mouth landed on her face in a flurry as I slammed her head into the wall again and again. "Stop fucking putting your hands on me!"

"I'm sorry. . . . I'm sorry. . . . I can't breathe . . . Aric . . . I can't . . ."

Before she passed out I let her limp body fall to the floor. I caught myself just in time. I'd told her ass over and over to stop putting her hands on me. Why she couldn't adhere to that, I didn't know. I left her there, on the floor in fetal position, clutching her neck, and crying.

By the time I'd made it to Chyanne's house, it was after Gabe and I had downed a few shots of Trago Tequila
and a few shots of Don Julio too. Gabe had a few warn-
ing shots for me after I told him what had happened
between me and Stephanie. I expected him too. He's
her brother, even though she treated him like he wasn't
shit, he still had her back to a certain extent. I was tipsy
enough to let him do it and get away with it. Had too
much shit on my mind. Like what I had done to my wife.
I was so pissed that I'd gotten a ticket for doing ninety
in a fifty-five-miles-per-hour zone. Stephanie had pissed
me off that badly; so pissed that I sat in my garage and
beat the hell out of my steering wheel for a good minute
or two because of what I had done to her. I wished like
hell she wouldn't make me put my hands on her. I didn't
want to but she insisted on pushing me to my limit! I
could only take so much and no matter how many times
I had told her that, she still didn't get it.

As I sat in Chyanne's driveway and thought, something akin to heartache overtook me. For so many years
I'd tried to cope with the physical altercations Stephanie and I had and each time they'd left me with a void
in my heart. It was thirty minutes after midnight and I
realized I had been sitting there a while when Chyanne
opened her door and called my name. She shielded
her eyes and yelled something at me. I couldn't hear
her because of the rain pouring down. When noticing
I couldn't hear her she closed the front door and went
back inside.

I sat there and thought about how every time something like me having to physically put my hands on
Stephanie happened, it always took me a while to get
my thought process back on point. So many issues in
our marriage that we'd never dealt with were now coming back to the surface. For a while living in the house

together back in New York felt as if we were living in a war zone. She'd cheat. I'd get mad. We would fight, have sex, and make up. I'd cheat. She'd get mad, confront the woman. We'd fight, have sex, and make up. I was to the point in my life where I just wanted peace. I'd gotten tired of the same dance and I hated like hell that I'd given her the impression that we could once again work it out. That's why I'd gone back to New York over the holidays. I just needed to see if she was where I wanted to be. I needed to know that it was over. So one last time I tried and one last time I got the answer that I wanted. It was over.

Chyanne knocked on my window and jarred me back to reality. I realized she was standing outside in the rain with a light jacket, some cotton shorts, tennis shoes, and a big black umbrella.

Wondering how long she'd been standing there I let the window down and asked, "Why are you out here in the rain?"

"Because you've been sitting out here with your headlights shining through the front of my house for about thirty minutes."

"Go in the house. I'll be in. Give me a minute."

I could tell she had been asleep. Her voice was soft and sweet while her eyes carried a blushful ambiance. They lured me in as I stared at her intently for a while.

She blushed under my observation before asking, "Are you coming in or are you just going to sit here?"

"Go in the house," I said a bit harsher than I intended to. She looked perplexed because of my tone but slowly turned away and made her way back inside.

About ten minutes later, I raced to her front door as the rain drenched me. It was coming down hard and felt as if each pelt was trying to break skin. Since I didn't want to walk wet across her snow white carpet, I took my shoes and clothes off at her door. I had no idea she had been standing there watching me as I looked up at her and she held her hand out for my wet clothes. I handed them to her.

"I laid a T-shirt and a pair of PJ's on the bed. You left them here before. I washed them."

She stood there and stared at me for a while. Looking at my face, probably drawing assumptions about what'd happened.

"I'll wash these and dry them for you," she said after a while tucking my clothes underneath her right arm.

Turning, she went toward her laundry room. Her wife beater was a little wet from standing in the rain and her cotton shorts hung to her back side giving me a good view of the jiggle it gave as she walked. I made my way to the bathroom in her bedroom and hopped into the shower, needing the hot water and steam to take my mood and my temper down a level. Once I was done with that, I walked into her bedroom and found the clothes she had laid out for me. I could smell her cooking something and my stomach immediately reminded me that I hadn't eaten in a couple of hours.

By the time I walked into the kitchen she was sautéing some seasoned chicken breast in olive oil. In the light she got a better look at my face and gasped. I didn't even bother to look in the mirror before I got in the shower and didn't bother to look after the water had burned my face, chest, and the back of my neck. She pulled a plate from the microwave as I sat down at the table. The silence around us spoke loudly, but I felt at peace being with her as she set a chicken sandwich and a plate of wild rice in front of me with the sliced tomatoes, pickles, lettuce, and condiments on the side. I ate it in silence while she finished cooking the last piece of chicken. I watched as she wrapped it and placed the plate in the microwave.

"I'll fix you another sandwich if you're still hungry after you finish," she said as she placed a cold glass of ice tea in front of me and sat down at the table with me. "Aric?" She called to me.

I looked over at her and finished chewing my food before answering. "What?"

"You get into a fight?"

Her question would have annoyed me if the look of genuine concern that covered her face didn't touch me.

"You can say that," I answered before putting a spoonful of rice in my mouth not wanting to divulge the details.

"Was it a cat that got a hold of you?" She asked playfully as she raised her eyebrows and smirked.

Although I didn't want to, I gave a little smirk of my own. "You can say that too."

There was silence again before she said, "I just wanted to make you smile. You seemed to be out of it. I don't think I like to see you look that way."

I squinted my eyes to look at her because I didn't have my glasses on and my eyes were stressed. She was indeed a beautiful young woman and I'd found myself intrigued by her the first moment I'd laid eyes on her. An innocent baby face surrounded by high cheek bones set off by big beautiful doe like eyes and she was thick. Plus sized is what America called her. I called it thickness. She was thick in all of the right places. Maybe that's why it was so hard to get her out my system. Maybe that's why I didn't want to get her out of my system.

"Don't worry about me. I'm fine. Are you ready for tomorrow?" I asked her.

"As ready as I'll ever be. I'm a little nervous . . . scared. My doctor says this could cause a lot of stress to me and the baby."

I finished the last little bit of the rice and sandwich before wiping my mouth with the paper towel. "I need to know. I know this will be a risk, but I have to know if it's my baby you're carrying."

She didn't say anything as she stood, and took the used dishes to the kitchen. She washed them and placed them in the dishwasher before walking to her front room and plopping down on her sofa. Picking up the remote she turned the TV on.

"I talked to Stephanie," I told her.

"Did she tell you what happened?"

"Some of it," I nodded as I stood and walked to stand in front of her. She sat looking up at me from the sofa with the remote in her hand. "Yeah. . . . Who was it that you were at lunch with today?"

My eyes raked her over and then I looked directly into her eyes. Looking into her eyes gave me a sense of power because of the way she cowered under my gaze. I could tell she was thinking about whether or not she should lie to me before she answered. Her lying to me had never been in her best interest. I stood wide legged with my arms folded across my chest, scratching my chin watching as she put the TV on mute and placed the remote on the table.

"I . . . . It was Jamie."

She cringed when I moved one of my arms to wipe one hand down my face. I frowned and asked, "What are you jumping for?"

She shrugged and I could see her visibly relax after a while. The look on her face told me she thought I was about to hit her. Seeing that look on her face took my anger over her being with Jamie down a level.

"Any particular reason you were with Jamie?" I asked her.

"Figured I should let him know that it was a very small possibility that he could be the father of this child."

I raised my eyebrows and titled my head to look at her. "Thought you were sure it was mine."

"I am, but . . . I'm just saying. If by chance that it isn't, he's the only other man . . ."

She stopped talking when she realized that I wasn't too keen on what I was hearing.

"I'm sure the baby is yours Aric. I just want to cover all of my bases."

The look she was giving me showed nervousness as well as guilt. I didn't say anything else about it and took her for her word as I let it go. Issues with my marriage were still clogging my mind.

"I stopped by to make sure you were okay with everything tomorrow," I said after a moment.

She exhaled. "Like I said I'm as ready as I'll ever be."

I was about to try to say something to calm her spirits, but my phone rang reminding me that I'd left it on the table by the door. It was Stephanie and I knew she wasn't going to stop calling until I answered, which I wasn't planning on doing anytime soon.

"Want me to get that for you?" Chyanne asked noticing I wasn't going to move from the spot I was in.

"No. Let it ring."

The rain was coming down hard and the wind was making the trees in Chyanne's front yard whip against her window panes. Once my phone stopped ringing Chyanne's home phone started. She quickly went to retrieve it and held it out to me as it continued to ring in her hand.

"It's your wife," she spat out. "How did she get my number?"

I ignored her outstretched hand. "More than likely from my phone. Let it ring," I told her again.

We both listened as her voicemail picked up and a few seconds later Stephanie's voice came through.

"I know he's there and I know you both hear the phone ringing. Tell him to pick up his phone!"

Stephanie's voice sounded high-pitched and discombobulated as I stood in the middle of the floor and listened to her. I could hear the hurt through the anger in her voice and whereas at one time that would have bothered me, but after what had happened earlier, I had no idea the feelings I still had for her. I'd said earlier that I didn't know who started cheating first, but it was all coming back to me now. She'd hurt me that first time, humiliated me because the man she was cheating with had been in my house on several occasions. She'd made me feel like a fool and all of the hurt and anger I'd pushed to the back of my mind was starting to resurface.

So when Chyanne finally picked up her phone and looked at me before answering, "He's not here." I didn't say a word.

"Don't lie for him you stupid cunt!" Stephanie yelled. Because Chyanne's answering machine had come on already I could still hear Stephanie loud and clear. "Put him on the phone," Stephanie demanded.

"I told you he wasn't here," Chyanne calmly lied again.

"You're a stupid bitch. You know that? What? Do you think you're special or something because he has enough power over you to make you lie for him? As soon as he finishes sticking his dick inside of you he's going to come right home and do the same thing to me.

So he's fucking you, and I'm fucking him . . . stupid ass
. . . I know he's there Chyanne! Put him on the phone
you fat ass whore!"

Chyanne held the phone out to me. I took it from her
hand and hung it up. Stephanie called back three or
four times and left nasty messages on her phone each
time. After a while she turned her ringer off. She didn't
say anything else to me as she turned and walked into
her bedroom. I didn't feel like going home and since I
knew that Chyanne was adamant about not having sex
with me anymore, I laid in her front room on the sofa
for a while. I couldn't sleep because I had too many
things going on in my head. Mix that with the hard rain
falling down and there was me, restless.

My body was talking to me. Dick was throbbing, aching. I could hear Chyanne moving around in her room
wishing I could go in there and have sex with her like
it was my last time seeing her. Images of me slamming
Stephanie's head into the wall kept flashing across my
mind like lightning across the sky. I hadn't meant to go
that far, but she kept pushing me. Times like then were
when I wished I could call my father and talk with him,
but anytime I called him my mother would want to talk
to me. I was never too keen on speaking with her unless
I absolutely had to.

Looking at the time, I decided it was time for me
to be headed home. Although I wasn't quite sure the
weather would permit it, I would try anyway. Knowing
that Stephanie would be up when I got in was another
tempting reason to stay right where I was. Judging by
how many times she had called my phone, I knew she
was still awake and I was betting she would be the first
thing I saw when I walked in the door. After putting my
clothes and shoes on, I knocked on Chyanne's bedroom
door to let her know I was leaving. When I didn't get

an answer I opened the door and saw that she was in her bathroom. I could see the light peeking from under the bathroom door and the shadows of her feet moving around. Opening the door she walked out just as I was about to yell that I was leaving.

She looked over at me through hooded eye lids. "I'm about to leave," I said.

She looked at the window and back to me before closing the bathroom door and moving so that I could fully see her body. She only had on the cotton shorts and her full breasts jiggled a bit before she moved her hand to cover herself from me. I could see that she'd forgotten she was top naked.

"Are you sure you want to go out there in this?" She asked. "You're free to sleep on the couch if you would like."

"No, but I have to be at the office in about three hours. It's two-thirty. If I leave now I can at least try to get a nap in before I have to get up."

She looked me up and down before crawling back into bed. Her ample ass in the air made my dick stir around in my pants at the thought of being behind her with a handful of her ass in my hand. When she had gotten comfortable and pulled the sheet to cover her she spoke up.

"Be safe. Will I hear from you tomorrow?"

"Of course you will. Call me when you're about to go in and when you leave out. I've already had my mouth swabbed earlier today so it's all on you now."

I watched her yawn and nod. "Lock the door. You still have the keys."

"Talk to you tomorrow," I told her.

I kept seeing her breasts jiggle in my head and wanted to give them a firm squeeze, wanted to do the same to her ass. I was yearning to be between her thighs right then. As I walked to the front door all I could think about was how her pussy hugged me when I was inside of her and how good that shit felt. Damn! I opened the door and quickly closed it back. No way in hell I would be able to leave without finding my way inside of her. I threw my keys, wallet, and watch on her sofa, kicked my shoes off and started to make my way back to her room.

"Aric," she called out.

I could hear her getting up and when she rounded the corner and saw me coming toward her, the look on her face said it all. She didn't try to hide her beautiful breasts from me this time. Her nipples called out to me as my hands immediately reached out to touch them, rubbing the pad of my thumb over each of her nipples. She hissed and moaned low in her throat. I closed the gap between us and brought her lips to mine. We both melted into one another. I could tell by the way she pulled my shirt over my head that there would be no stopping tonight. Picking her up, she wrapped her thighs tightly around me as I carried her to the bed and laid her down. For a second or two I just looked at her as she looked up at me. I didn't even know where I wanted to start kissing her body.

Quickly stepping out of my pants and boxer briefs, I kneeled before her deciding that I wanted to start with her beautiful thick chocolate thighs. I easily slid her short shorts off. Chyanne's body excited me like no other woman I had ever been with and as soon as my lips touched her inner thigh, she arched and moaned. I loved her instant reaction to me. I licked and kissed all the way up to those creases in between her legs, licking and kissing around the slick piece of flesh that was calling out to me, as she arched and tried to put my mouth where she longed for it to be.

My dick thumped at her sounds, dancing to the tune of Chyanne as I kissed up and down her inner thighs, giving her a little tease of nibbles and kisses before I went to put my lips and tongue where I really wanted them to be. The rain drowned out her whimpers of pleasure creating a sensual atmosphere around us as I kissed a trail up her thighs until I reached her center. She was so wet I could smell it. Her scent ignited more fire within me. Smelled like the freshest earthiest musky scent. I was thinking that I was going to tease her a little more, but before I could help myself, I closed my mouth around her slick mound and rubbed my face in her juices. The more she arched and moaned, the more she brought her essence into my mouth. I'd missed that shit, missed her sweet taste and missed the way her body reacted to me, missed her syrupy sweetness racing down the back of my throat.

She excited me with the way she threw her pussy in my face as she twisted and turned grabbing both sides of my face to pull me closer. I obliged her and tried to smother myself in her juices, rubbing my entire face in it again using my tongue to lap up her juices and to pleasure her swollen core. Thunder and lightning ripped across the skies lighting up the room just enough so I could see her head thrown back. Seeing one of her hands go to her breasts I figured I was jealous and decided I wanted to taste and feel them as well. Licking the rest of her wetness from my lip while she caressed my bald head, I came up between her thighs and caged her in with both my arms on the sides of her. She looked up at me; she had moisture in her eyes. Not crying, but I'd learned anytime she was turned on her eyes watered. Before taking her right nipple into my mouth, I held eye contact with her. I loved the look she gave me. Chyanne made a man feel like he was in complete control of her.

She was completely submissive to me when it came to sex and that shit got my dick hard like nothing else.

"You miss me?" I asked her, just to make her wait for what I knew she wanted a little while longer.

"I do," she all but whispered.

As I leaned down to take her left nipple in my mouth, I guided my head a few inches inside of her. She didn't know what to do. She half moaned, half screamed, and then called on God—shit got me high like I was on drugs.

"Oh . . . God Aric . . ."

Her pussy was still as tight as it was the first time I'd had sex with her. It was hot, wet, and tight enough to drive any man crazy. I took my time loving her breasts. I kissed around her nipples and areolas before kissing around her whole soft and creamy chocolaty breast. Did that with each one, as I slowly slid my way inside of her inch. . . . by. . . . inch. It felt so good that I just had to lay there for a minute.

"Damn Chyanne! Why does this shit have to be so good?"

I asked that more to myself than to her. I hadn't even fully allowed myself to enter her yet and I could feel my dick throbbing for release already while her breathing became erratic and her nails dug into my back. She brought her legs up higher as she arched and called my name. I slid in a little further.

"You want it?" I asked her.

She nodded frantically. "Please . . ."

I brought my lips down to hers and her tongue sought mine like she was famished for it. She moaned and it traveled down my throat and settled in the pit of my stomach. Right then I pushed myself past her tightness and embedded myself deep within her sugar walls. She let out a scream of passion that filled the room as her eyes rolled to the back of her head.

"Damn, baby, this shit feels good." I told her.

I could feel her cream coating my dick as I skillfully thrust in and out of her. Her insides inhaled and exhaled against my hardness making me let out a breath I didn't know I was holding. At that moment I lost myself inside of her good loving. Something about this woman's sex drove me out of my mind. My nails gripped her thighs as I pushed them farther back and grooved in and out of her like her body was my life line. Chyanne moaned, sang my name, scratched my back, and threw her pussy back at me full speed ahead. Everything I'd taught her she was showcasing it to me. I must say that as the teacher, I was beyond pleased.

"That's right baby, work that shit," I said in her ear as I let my tongue graze it before biting down on her neck causing her to moan and shiver against me again.

I could tell when she was about to come. Her walls gripped me tighter and her movements became frantic as the muscles in the back of my legs tightened. When I knew she was about to release I intertwined our hands together just as I brought my mouth down on hers to drown out her screams. Our tongues danced with each others as my dick grew harder and when I felt her release, it was only minutes later that I did the same. Releasing all of my aggression inside of her, I pumped and pumped until I was sure I'd released all I had inside of her.

So my weight wouldn't hurt her, I fell over beside her. We lay silent like that until she fell asleep in my arms. I lay there a while and thought on how to go about getting my wife to sign the divorce papers so we could both move on with our lives. I don't know what happened between the times she had wanted a divorce up until recent, but I was wishing like hell I would have given her a divorce when she asked for one. After a while I got up, took a quick shower and prepared to leave. I tried to wake Chyanne to tell her I was leaving, but she was sprawled out across the bed sleeping like a baby. I pulled the covers over her and made sure to lock the door on my way out.

Chyanne

Sitting in that doctor's office waiting for my name to be called was the most nerve wrecking thing I'd ever done. If I hadn't been afraid of Aric's reaction, I would have left about three times. Since he had gone the day before to the DNA center and had his mouth swabbed, it was all on me. As I lay on that table and waited for the testing to begin, nervousness settled in. I got so scared that maybe I wouldn't be able to see my child come into the world. That scared me more than anything. I never even knew the possibility of being a mother would affect me in a way that made me want to cry at the thought of a miscarriage. All kinds of scenarios ran through my mind as the doctor read off the risks involved in what I was about to get done.

But, it was done. The test had been done and Aric had paid for it to be expedited so we would know the results in one to three days. Not long after leaving the doctor's office, I texted Aric to let him know the deed was done. I was so shocked when he sent me back a *'Thank you'* and a smiley face that all I could do was smile. I was feeling so caught up in emotions that I sent him back an *'I love you'* and when he replied *'Ditto'* it made my day!

The hardest part for me was over and I was glad about it. It kind of felt like a weight had been lifted and I could move on to more important things like getting my guest room cleaned out for the baby. When I had awakened that morning, I had stood in the mirror for a good fifteen minutes promising my child that I would be the best mother on the planet. I'm not even sure if he or she could hear me yet, but I wanted it to be known.

Waves of excitement would wash over me at times and then those same waves would turn into nervousness and anxiety. Whenever I had flashes of my childhood my mood would become sullen. That day I was about to do something I hadn't done since I was eighteen. I remembered what happened that day like it was nothing.

I had just walked across the stage as Valedictorian and looked out into the audience. I still didn't see my mother and I had a feeling that her and my father had gotten into another fight. My mom had never missed anything I'd ever participated in at school. Even when my dad had blackened both of her eyes and her face was swollen beyond recognition, she would still show up after she'd tried her best to hide the bruises. I'd look out and there she would be, smiling and waving, but she wasn't there that day, my graduation day. I knew something was wrong and as soon as the chief of police and a few other officers walked into the gymnasium, I knew they had come for me. I had just shaken the principle's hand and was making my way across the stage when I saw one of my classmates pointing toward me. I took my cap off and raced off of the stage to meet them halfway.

"Are you Chyanne Johnson?" the chief asked me.

I nodded and tried to keep the tears at bay. "Yes . . . yes I am. What's going on?"

"Come with us," was all he said as all of my peers watched me being escorted out of my graduation.

My heartbeat was fast and hard. It was hard for me to breathe as I sat in the back of the Chief's car and looked out at nothing as we took the scenic route to my house. My stomach plummeted as I took in the site. The scene in front of my house looked like something out of a crime drama; police cars, news cameras, and yellow crime scene tape. I jumped out of the car before it stopped moving. My blue graduation gown got stuck onto something on the door of the car and I tore it as I tried to run toward the entrance of my house. I could see blood strewn across the front room before I made it up the front steps.

"Mom!"

I called out to her as I frantically searched the house. I ran to the kitchen, back to the front room, and then the den.

"Mom!"

"Calm down," an officer said to me as he tried to grab me.

I dodged his grasp and ran for the den. I saw blood pooling around the door as I pushed it open and saw police surrounding a body. I screamed and kicked as I tried to get through the blockade of bodies shielding the body lying lifeless under a white sheet. That was the day I lost both my parents.

"Mom," I shouted again, hoping she would show her face and calm my fears.

I screamed, cried, and yelled for her but she didn't answer me. That morning she'd told my father that she was leaving. She had packed only a few things and we'd both almost escaped the house, but my dad came through the door as we were leaving. As soon as he saw the bags in our hands he lost it. First he back handed her so hard she went flying across the room. I tried to grab him and keep him off of her to no avail. My dad was a big and tall man; six feet nine inches tall and built like a brick wall. Not an inch of fat *anywhere in sight. His coffee brown eyes had turned into slits it seemed and his face was twisted in anger. I grabbed his arm as he basically dragged me across the room to get to my mother. I'd seen my dad lose it before, but this time was different. Something in the air told me that day would be different.*

Horns blared in the distance and snapped me back into reality. When I looked up from my thoughts I was in Sherwood Memorial Park cemetery. Tears were flooding my eyes as I realized I was crying uncontrollably. I thought I could go out there and go see one of my parents, but I couldn't bring myself to get out of my car. I sat there for about thirty minutes before I decided to leave. It had been seven years and I still wasn't ready to face my past. I made a u-turn and turned out back into traffic, trying to get away from that place as quickly as I could.

After realizing I didn't want to go home just yet, I drove down Mt. Zion and ended up at Babies "R" Us. I figured shopping for the baby would take my mind off of things. Thinking on it, I hadn't really been out of the house to do too much of anything. I'd paid a few bills on line and looked into some information on furthering my education, but that was it. So shopping for the baby would be therapeutic for me.

I had been in the store for about thirty minutes picking up little things here and there. Since I didn't know the sex of the baby just yet, I picked up neutral things like all white onesies, a few packs of socks, booties, some newborn diapers, and a few pacifiers. I couldn't even explain the jubilance I was feeling in that moment. I heard a female voice calling my name. I turned and looked at the woman as she was approaching me. She looked familiar, but I couldn't place her. She looked Hispanic as her curly honey blonde pony tail swung behind her. She had a vibrant smile on her face.

"Hey Chyanne," she greeted as she got closer and held her hand out for me to shake.

I sat my purse in the cart and shook her hand.

"Hello," I greeted still trying to place her face.

"You don't remember me do you?"

We both laughed when I shook my head.

"I'm sorry, but no, I don't, and I'm no good with names and faces."

"I'm Shelley. We met a couple of months ago . . ."

"Ohhh. Okay, now I remember."

She was the woman who Gabriel had been talking to the night April had slapped me when Aric had invited me to that social event with him.

She smiled. "Yeah. I know I may look a little different, but I'm here shopping with my sister for my niece that will be here soon," she smiled as she talked.

"Congratulations," I told her, still wondering if there was a reason for her to be talking to me. Last I remembered she was getting a kick out of April humiliating me in front of everyone.

"Look, I'm glad I ran into you. I know the last time we met was not under the best of circumstances, but I asked Aric about you and he said you no longer worked for him."

I nodded. "Long story."

She lightly touched my arm and waved her hand. "Trust me, when dealing with Aric it's always a long story, but that's neither here nor there. I'm about to open my own marketing and advertising firm and I'm looking for a partner as well as people to work for me," she said as she opened her purse and pulled out a business card and held it out for me to take.

I took the card while she continued talking, "All Aric used to talk about was how good you were at what you did. I'm really looking for a strong all female team to start out with me and I would be thrilled if you would think about the possibility."

I looked at the card for a second thinking that I did need a job. I'd been planning on talking to Aric later to see if I could have my old job back. She must have picked up on my hesitation.

"Look, I'm not asking you to make any decisions now, but please think about it and get back to me by the end of the week. I'm trying to get things up and running soon and would love to have you on."

"Okay, I'll think on it and let you know something soon."

She smiled again and looked at her ringing phone. "That's all I ask," she said. "Call me anytime."

I watched her as she walked off, thinking about the fact that I indeed needed a job, but I thought Aric would give me my job back knowing that I was pregnant and would need one with another mouth to feed. I stuck her card in my purse not even sure if I would make use of it and finished shopping, ending up spending way over five hundred dollars. Yeah, I went a little baby crazy.

I pulled into my neighborhood feeling a little better. I'd put my past demons behind me for the moment and couldn't wait to get into the house to sleep. At least I was feeling happy until I saw April's black Nissan Altima in my driveway. The car was parked to the side so it was easy for me to pull around it and park in front of my garage. I sat in my car for a while thinking about how I was not ready to deal with her yet. I hadn't seen or spoken to her since I found out Aric had sex with her. I sat there and shook my head thinking about all the mess that had transpired between her and me over the last couple of months. I should have listened when Justin told me to watch her, but I'm the one to always see the good in everyone.

Anger got a strong hold on me and my heart rate sped up as I thought about all the things that I'd done for April and her kids. The kids I didn't mind helping, but the things April had said and done to me were unforgiveable in my book. I had pushed the anger so far to the back of my mind that, at times, I'd forgotten about it; didn't want to deal with it. I exhaled and stepped out of my car leaving the bags inside because I didn't want her to know I was pregnant. Knowing her, she would judge me harshly and call me stupid in every language she knew.

The driver-side door opened as soon as I closed my door and April stepped out. She had her purse in the crease of her right arm, her denim hip huggers were almost too tight, and her hair had grown out into a longer, but still short style. The chocolate-wedged shoes she had on gave more definition to her legs and her sweater midriff showed off her belly ring. There was an awkward silence between us and I found myself wanting to slap spit from her mouth.

"Hey Chy," she spoke.

I folded my arms across my chest and responded. "April."

She chuckled and clucked her tongue to the roof of her mouth while shaking her head.

"I came by because I figured it was time we talked."

"About what exactly?"

She looked at me as if I had asked a stupid question.

"Look, I know you're still probably mad about the whole Aric thing, but the way I figure it, he wasn't your man to begin with . . . at least to my knowledge he wasn't. I asked him what was going on between you two and he never gave me a straight answer. All he was to me was a good fuck. So you should be mad at him, not me."

The way she smirked while she talked and the attitude in her voice unnerved me. I kept my composure. Everything was always a game to April and she always had to come out on top. I had too much going on to be wasting my time allowing her to get me upset.

"How many times did you sleep with him?" I asked.

She shrugged. "Maybe four, five times."

I could lie and tell you her answer didn't bother me, but it felt like I had been sucker punched in the stomach. Switching my weight from one foot to the other I stared at her . . . hard.

"Look, Chyanne, it's not like you told me y'all had something going on," she said switching her purse from one side to the other.

"But you knew."

"How was I supposed to know? I'm not a fucking mind reader."

"You knew, April and I know you knew. I could tell by the smirk on your face when I caught him at your house."

"Girl, he wasn't even your man. If he was, he wasn't the four or five times we fucked. The point is, you should be mad at him not me."

The attitude level in her voice had gone up a notch and her defensiveness almost made me laugh . . . almost. I shook my head and chuckled.

"I don't know what your purpose was for coming over here April. I don't know if it was because you wanted to apologize, or to see how much more you could try to break me down. I have no idea what our friendship was ever made of. All you have ever done is treated me like I was less than you were. You insulted me at every chance and all you did was take from this friendship. You never gave."

"What?" she asked almost as if she couldn't believe what I had said. Her face was twisted in a sneer. "Are you fucking serious right now? Chyanne, who was there for you when you found out your ex was cheating on you?"

"April please," I said and chuckled, although there was nothing funny about the way I was feeling at the moment. "Who was there for you when your parents died? Who was there for you when Jonathon started cheating on you? Who was there for you when you lost your last child? Who was there for your ass when Jonathon walked out and left you? Me. No damn body, but me! Who paid your damn mortgage a couple of months ago? Me. Who paid your car note up for six months so you could catch up? Me. Exactly what have you done for me, huh?"

I was so loud that I scared myself when I realized it, so imagine the look on her face. "I didn't ask you to do shit for me!"

"You didn't have to. That's what friends are for, but you're too damn stuck on yourself to get that."

"Bitch please. I always carried your fat ass around—

Before I knew what I was doing, I had slapped her down to the ground and she fell hard. She tried to get up and I slapped her again. Open-handed slaps . . . as hard as I could give her. Tears stung my eyes and I slapped her again for good measure. She started swinging her arms wildly and tried to grab me to no avail. I stepped back and allowed her to get up. She dropped her purse and decided she wanted to come for me again, but I shoved her so hard she fell back against the grill of her car. Her face grimacing in pain as the wind got knocked out of her.

"Get the hell out of my driveway April. I've been nothing but a friend to you," I said through tears and

I had to wipe spit from my mouth. "All I ever did was try to help you and those boys and all you've ever done was treat me like crap. No more. Get the hell out of my driveway and I won't say it again. And just for the record, Aric is married. So we both played the fool."

Too late, I realized my neighbors were looking on. I snatched my purse and keys off the trunk of my car and looked back at April one last time. Tears stained her reddened face and for some reason I felt bad for what I had just done. I had just lost the only person that I had left. I jammed my keys into my front door to unlock it and slammed the door so hard that a couple of vases fell over on the end table nearest the door. I plopped down on the couch and I cried. I cried for both the parents that I had lost; cried for the friend I thought I had . . . a friend that I lost. I cried because, for the first time, I realized that I was really all alone.

I cried myself to sleep and woke up a few hours later to my phone ringing. At first it startled me and I jumped up from my couch like someone was after me. Once I realized it wasn't my cell phone, I raced to my house phone in my bedroom and by the time I picked up my answering machine had come on.

"Just wanted you to know that when he finished fucking you, I fucked him."

At first I had to grip my mind around who was on the other end of that message. When it came to me I shook my head and stood with arms folded trying to understand what would make a grown woman play on another woman's phone. I could hear my cell phone beeping signaling me that I had text messages. There was another message from her. That one telling me to stay away from her husband or she would whoop my ass. I guess she meant like she'd done the last time, right? I laughed to myself and picked up my cell phone. I had several text messages from a number I didn't know.

I opened the first one and almost dropped my phone. It was a video of Aric and his wife having sex. I didn't know what to do, or what to say, at first, as I watched her ride Aric as her life depended on it. The only saving grace was that I didn't look at it long enough to see if Aric was enjoying it or not. I quickly erased it and looked at the next message. It was a picture of Aric's manhood and he was fully aroused. The message underneath the picture read *"I already had the dick for the day, now it's your turn."* I erased that one and another popped up. The next picture was of her posed naked in the same bathroom that I had been in countless times while I was at his house.

Her body was flawless. She was the standard of beauty according to America. Underneath that picture the message read, *"You know you're no competition so stop playing yourself!☺"* I didn't know if I wanted to laugh or scream and punch a few walls. How did I find myself fighting with a woman about a husband I didn't know she had? Why was she wasting all of her time sending me things so intimate to my phone? Seeing her and Aric having sex gave me a sinking feeling in the pit of my stomach. I mean I wasn't stupid. I figured that he'd been having sex with his wife, but I don't know. I guess I wasn't prepared to see it full frontal. So not only did I have to deal with the fact that he and April carried on a sexual relationship, I had to deal with his and his wife's sex life being thrown in my face as well.

Aric had such a strong hold on my heart. Don't ask me why. I couldn't help who I fell in love with. I figured there'd be plenty who would think that I was dumb for even falling in love with Aric, but the man got into my mind first. He took care of me when I was sick, bought things for me, made me feel special at times. We spent a hell of a lot of time together. Yes, there were times when he acted an ass. There was the time that . . . that incident happened in his office when Gabe and I went to lunch. Aric didn't like that so he pulled me into his hide-a-way office and to this day I don't even know what to call what happened. He'd sat me on the desk and roughly taken me sexually. It wasn't until I cried out that he was hurting that he stopped. I hated to even thinking about that. Then there was the time he backhanded me across my bed. But, to me, his good had outweighed his bad until his wife showed up and a couple of those times I think I provoked him. Yes, I said I think I provoked Aric at times when he showed his ass. I mean he had told me on several occasions what he liked and what he didn't like and at times I did things he didn't like.

I'd missed five calls from Aric. I knew that sometimes he'd stay up late working so I took my chances on returning his phone call. As I looked at the clock I realized I had slept longer than I thought I had. It was a little after midnight. If his wife had answered the phone, I'd already made up my mind to hang up on her. Aric and I had sex the night before and although when I woke up I felt bad about it, I couldn't deny that it was mind blowing. Aric knew what to say, what to do, and I finally found out what that spot was that everyone kept talking about. I'd found that out the first time I'd had sex with him. I didn't know what made me go there with him again. It could have been the mood. It could have been because I was horny. It could have been because Aric was so sexy to me and I couldn't resist him. His body was the stuff that girls like me could only dream of. Or, it could have been because I needed to prove to myself that, no matter what his wife said, he still wanted me. In a sense, I wanted her to feel us having sex so she would know that no matter how many fat bitches she called me, her husband still wanted me.

The phone rang three times. She answered. I hung up. I called right back and she answered again. I hung up again. The next time I called back the phone went right to voice mail. She'd turned his phone off. I smiled and shook my head. If it wasn't so late I would have driven to his house and used the key to let myself in. Yeah, I was being evil and vindictive, but the woman annoyed me to no end and I was still pissed about her putting her hands on me, threatening to take my child away from me, and about all the mess she had sent to my phone.

With a devious smirk on my face, I dialed the home phone. He answered.

"Hey, you called?"

"Yeah," he answered.

Either he was sleeping or he was tired. His voice still washed over me and melted my insides.

"What the hell were you doing that you missed my call five times?" he asked me with a little attitude in his voice that made me smile.

"I was sleep."

"Yeah, right. How'd the testing go?"

"Everything went well. I feel fine."

"Did they say when the results would be in?"

I sat down on the side of my bed thinking of how sexy he sounded on the phone. No matter what this man had done, I couldn't break whatever hold he had on me and I wished like hell I could.

"Didn't you pay for one to three day results?"

He chuckled a bit and it traveled through the phone through my ear and settled in my stomach.

"Don't be a smart ass Chyanne. It isn't becoming of you."

I heard his wife in the background. "It's after twelve in the damn morning Aric. What the hell could be an emergency at this time of morning? Is she in labor? Is she having a miscarriage? The fat bitch could have said something when I answered your phone instead of hanging up!"

It was a while before he said anything and I imagined him giving her the same look he gave me when I annoyed him.

"Get the hell out of my office with that shit Stephanie," he told her.

Something else was said but it was muffled as it sounded like the phone dropped and I couldn't really hear what was going on. I heard her yell something and then a door slam. There was a lot of noise as he picked the phone back up.

"Hello," he answered.

"Yeah. I'm sorry, I didn't mean to cause any trouble."

"What did you think calling here at this time of night would cause? A party?"

I was silent. I wasn't expecting him to say that.

"I'm sorry," I finally said. "I called your cell—"

"Yeah. Don't worry about it. What's done is done? Do me a favor and try not to call the house phone unless you really need me."

My feelings were hurt. "Okay," was all I could say.

"Call my cell anytime you want. Just don't call here because I don't want to hear her mouth."

So there I had it. That devious feeling that I'd had earlier all but disappeared. He'd put me in my place about calling his home. His wife's happiness was more important to him than anything I had to say to him. I sat there like a child that had been chastised and picked at my fingernails feeling like a fool all over again.

"Chyanne?"

"What?"

He paused. "What the hell do you have an attitude for?"

"Nothing."

"What? Now you're mad at me too?"

I didn't say anything. I let my silence speak for me.

"So, now you don't have anything to say to me?" he asked. "The fuck are you mad at?" He yelled and it scared me.

That pissed me off and I hung up the phone. He called back four times and I ignored the calls. To ease my mind and to keep myself from going insane I started to clean. I vacuumed my front room, took a shower, and found a movie to watch. I was too worked up to sleep, had too much on my mind and I was about to make my way to bed anyway since there was nothing else to do when head lights in my driveway blinded me. Wondering who it was I was on my way to look out of the window when I heard a door slam and sat back down. I had a clue as to whom it would be and didn't even bother to look out of my window like I was going to do. A couple of seconds later Aric shoved my front door open.

"What the fuck you hang up on me for?" he asked as soon as he opened the door and it was so low in his throat that he sounded as if he growled it out. "And then you want to play games and not answer the phone when I call. What the hell is wrong with you?"

He still had on half of his suit from the work day; the black dress pants and a white wife beater, and his eyes were furious behind the black-framed Cartier glasses on his face.

"Apparently your wife was more important to you at the moment," I said before I could catch myself.

"Don't you go and start this shit with me ,Chyanne. Too late at night for bullshit."

"Didn't you drive over here this late at night for bullshit?" I countered with a little attitude clearly laced throughout my tone.

He balled his lips, exhaled, and looked pointedly at me. "Got something you want to say, Chyanne? Go ahead and get that shit off your chest and let this be the last time before I have to say something to you that would hurt your feelings."

I stood with the bowl of fruit I had in my hand and rolled my eyes at him on my way to the kitchen.

"Roll your eyes at me one more time."

I didn't respond to the lethal promise of the threat that went unspoken in his tone. Although I didn't think he would put his hands on me while I was pregnant, I wasn't going to try and test my theory. I put the bowl of fruit away and walked back to my couch to sit. His eyes were still watching me like he was an eagle watching his prey.

"You drove all the way over here to stand there and look at me?"

Aric scared me at times, but there was a defiance that sparked in me every time I thought about how he'd made me fall in love with him knowing he was married. The thought that he had used me made my eye twitch as we stared at each other. I knew I was seconds away from being snatched off of my sofa but, at that point, I didn't care.

"Go on and say what you have to say Chyanne," he snapped at me.

"Who said I had anything to say? You're the one who barged in here like you had a problem. I don't have a problem . . . oh, other than the fact that you forgot to mention you were married, had sex with April four or five times, and now I have to deal with being called a fat bitch every time I call your phone."

I gave a sarcastic half second smile and turned the volume back up on my TV. It was only five seconds before he snatched the remote and turned the TV off. He dropped the remote on the table and stood directly in front of me. I either had to look up at him or stare at his dick in my face. I chose to look up at his face.

"April?" he repeated it like a question and frowned. "We're back to talking about that bitch now?"

"Oh, now she's a bitch? She wasn't that when you were having sex with her!"

"What? I had sex with her once. She sucked my dick once. That's it. Last I heard she was giving Gabe the same treatment. She didn't mean shit to me. A quick fuck is all she was and I've been telling her the same thing I'm telling you every time she's called my phone. I'm quite sure I've told you this before . . ."

For some reason it made me feel a little better to hear him clarify things about him and April. Hearing her tell me that they'd had sex that many times unnerved me and made me feel as if she would always have one up on me when it came to Aric. So hearing him tell me one more time that she didn't mean anything to him solidified to me exactly what she'd meant to him, but that still left his wife to deal with.

"And what about your wife?" I asked folding my arms across my chest.

"What about her? Look, I have a wife. You're going to have to get used to that for now just like she's going to have to get used to the fact that if this is my baby, you'll always be around."

I cocked my head back to the side and looked at him like he was nuts. "I don't have to get used to anything!"

"You don't really have a choice now do you? As the mother of my child, it's imperative that you do. For the time being Stephanie isn't going anywhere."

"I didn't even know there was a damn Stephanie. In the world according to Aric, he didn't have to mention he had a wife until she sucker punched me," I snapped sardonically.

"I told you there was some shit that I had to handle—"

"Didn't say it was a wife."

He rubbed his left hand across his bald head and then down his face. "So that's it? You're mad about the wife."

It grated my nerves how he made it seem like him having a wife wasn't a big deal and how he seemed to negate my feelings on the matter.

"I'm mad about being put in the middle of something I had no idea there was! I'm mad because I have to deal with your childish wife sending videos of you and her having sex to my phone, pictures of your penis to my phone, and pictures of her naked to my phone. That's why I'm mad, Aric!"

"I get that, but what the hell are you made at me about it for? I didn't send that shit to your phone and I didn't know that she had sent it. Get your number changed if it bothers you that damn much. And I can promise you what she sent you of her and me having sex is something old she pulled up on her phone," he said.

"I shouldn't have to get my number changed because you can't control your wife! I didn't start this mess and I don't want to be in the middle of it anymore."

"So what does that mean?"

"That means I'm done."

I watched as he folded his arms across his chest, his thumb and pointing finger rubbing his chin before asking, "Done with what exactly?"

I knew what he was asking so I was trying to think of a pleasant way to say I was done with him. I couldn't think with his presence looming over me like he was a menacing giant. I tried to get up and he used his right hand to gently push me back down on the sofa. He leaned forward and both of his muscled arms caged me in, his face so close to mine that I could feel his breath on my nose.

"Done with what Chyanne?" He asked me again.

I felt my head spinning and my heart beating loudly as I looked up at him trying my best not to cower under his stare. His cologne usually turned me on, now it made me nauseous.

"I'm done with this Aric, with us. I don't want to fight another woman about her husband. It's not right on any level. I don't want to be your 'other' woman."

"Who said you had to be the other woman?"

"You made me the other woman when you . . ."

"When I what?"

A shiver ran through me. I'd told him I loved him in a text message, but I didn't know if I wanted to come out and tell him to his face. He was already making it hard for me to breathe being so close to me. I guess you could call me a sad case because, in that moment, it proved that he really had me shaken. I was afraid to express my feelings in my home.

"Do you really want to be done with me Chyanne?" He asked me.

"On that level, yes."

His stare was a lethal one. One that made me want to sink down into the couch and disappear. We kept playing the staring game until he stood and moved toward the door. He looked to be deep in thought as he opened my front door.

"That's cool Chyanne," he said after turning to me. "I'm not going to make you do anything you don't want to do, but make up your fucking mind. Don't play with me. One minute you don't want me to touch you and the next minute you got your legs spread for me telling me how good my dick is. Don't say shit else to me unless it's to tell me if the baby you're carrying is mine. I don't have time for games. I have enough bullshit to deal with at home and I'm not going to deal with yours too."

I didn't know why, but in that moment, it was like, I felt dreadful. I felt as if he was about to walk out of my life forever and I wasn't sure I wanted that. I mean, I did love him. As much as I hated to admit it, and as angry as I was at him for leading me on knowing he had a wife, I still wasn't sure if I didn't want him to be a part of my life. I know I'd said I wanted to be done just minutes before, but I didn't expect the reaction he'd given me. As he walked out of the door, I jumped from my couch and ran after him.

"Aric, wait!" I yelled, but he kept walking to his car.

I knew he saw me standing in my driveway and I knew he heard me calling him, but he ignored me and drove away. I was left standing there looking like a fool wondering if he was really done with me. I tried calling him several times that night—left several messages, but he didn't answer. That sinking feeling in the pit of my stomach that I always got. . . . yeah for the next couple of days it stayed with me. I couldn't get out of bed. I was sick. Not sure if it was from the pregnancy, or the thought that Aric would no longer be a part of my life if this baby wasn't his; although I knew it was his. I was throwing up again and was doing a horrible job of eating like I was supposed to.

Every time I tried to eat something it would come right back up. I ended up in the emergency room getting an IV drip in my arm because I'd dehydrated myself. I tried calling Aric to tell him, but either his wife answered his phone or he wouldn't answer. I called him at work and his assistant said he was busy anytime I got through.

Jamie came to take me home from the hospital because it was clear I couldn't drive myself, and he was the only person I had left to call. Justin was out of the country and even though I'm sure the pregnancy had something to do with my being sick, Jamie also knew it had something to do with Aric. He could tell by the way every time my phone rang and I jumped for it, or when he asked me why I didn't call Aric to come and get me. My reaction and tears were probably a dead giveaway. After telling me exactly what he thought of Aric, Jamie and I had a few disparaging words because, then, he proceeded to tell me in so many words how stupid he thought I was. Although we had that argument, Jamie still stayed with me until he had to get back to his work and I was grateful.

Two days after Aric walked out of my house, the test results came back.

Aric

A knock on the door silenced the conversation in the room.

"Yeah," I called out.

We all turned to see Stephanie walk in with food and beer. She'd been upstairs cooking and had been in a good mood ever since she found out that her father was coming to visit. Once her father had retired as Chief of Police for the county of Fulton, he and Stephanie's mother had moved to Nassau in the Bahamas. Gabe, Gabe's father, whose name was Xavier, and I had been sitting in my entertainment room playing Dominoes and talking about different things, including Stephanie and our marriage. Mr. Williams was an old-school cat. He was the type of Black man who would have been labeled distinguished back in the day and even today. He was dressed in what I was sure to be an expensive linen suit and his feet clad in men's Ostrich sandals showed he was a man of luxury. He was sixty-two but looked no older than thirty-five and he and Gabe looked like they could be brothers instead of father and son. They both had locs that stopped just below their shoulder blades and as far back as I could remember Mr. Williams had always kept his that length.

The smell of fried chicken hit our noses as well as the other food she and her mother had been cooking upstairs. The look on her face was euphoric as she smiled at her father. It would never be denied that Stephanie was a daddy's girl just as it wouldn't be denied that she had him wrapped around her pretty little fingers.

"I brought food," she exclaimed as she set a platter of fried chicken down on the bar behind us.

She kissed my lips. It was all for show I guess. She hadn't kissed me in days. Her mother was right behind her with a steaming pot that smelled like her famous broccoli casserole and I was sure more food was to follow. Just as Gabe and his father looked alike, Cecilia and Stephanie looked like spitting images of one another. They were both petite, had beautiful bodies, and their dark skin was without blemish. They both lived by Pilates and Cecilia still taught kick boxing at a domestic violence shelter. The only difference was that Stephanie's hair flowed down her back and Cecilia wore her once silky tresses in sister locs now.

"Good Lord, how do you all sit in here with all of this smoke?" Cecilia asked fanning her hand after she had set the pot down.

Mr. Williams favorite past time was smoking his Cuban cigars but the smoke didn't bother me or Gabe.

"If you would make your retreat hasty, you wouldn't have to worry about the smoke," Mr. Williams told her.

Although his words came out without fervor, Cecilia smiled. "I figure Xavier is talking about something they don't want us to hear Stephanie, so come on," she said while still smiling at her husband.

She was right. I guess Stephanie had called and told her parents about Chyanne or more so about Chyanne being pregnant. Now they were at my house and Mr. Williams was doing what any father would do for his daughter. He was trying to assess the situation and make sure she wasn't going to be out on her ass. I knew my wife and I knew by the way she was looking at her father that she was hoping he could help her to fix what used to be our marriage. I knew the reason she had called both her parents and I knew the reason her father was taking the time to sit in my basement and talk to me.

I watched as she and her mother made their way back up the stairs. Things between Stephanie and me had been okay for the last couple of days. There hadn't been any arguments and no fights. Probably because I hadn't been talking to Chyanne and I had been focused on my work more than anything. Chyanne had gotten on my damn nerves so bad the last time I'd seen her that my mind was made up to leave her the hell alone. I wasn't going to force anybody to do what they didn't want to do, so if she didn't want me to touch her in that way then I wouldn't. I was tired of her freely giving me pussy one minute and then acting like I was forcing her to do it the next. Shit got old and it got old real fast. I hadn't talked to her since that night although she had been calling like she had lost her mind.

Don't ask me about my feelings for Chyanne because I wouldn't be able to give you a straight answer. Did I like her? Yes. Did I care a hell of a lot about her? Yes. Did I love her? I had a whole lot of love for her and what she presented to me when I met her. Believe it or not, she was good for me when we first met. She gave me what I hadn't had in a long time. She gave me peace and tranquility. She gave me something different than what I was used to. Did I want to be with her? No. Once Stephanie and her mother had disappeared and closed the door, Gabe, Mr. Williams, and I went back to playing Dominoes.

"Okay, now that all of the bullshit talk is out of the way," Mr. Williams said as he put his cigar down and pushed his Dominoes to the side. "Tell me what the hell is going on with you, Stephanie, and whoever the hell this other woman is."

I looked over at him and made sure to keep eye contact. "Her name is Chyanne and there's nothing going on between me and Stephanie that hasn't been going on since before Chyanne was in the picture. I don't know why she keeps insisting that it has anything to do with her."

"Maybe it's because you got her pregnant," he answered quickly.

"Wasn't intentional."

"Did you use protection when you were fucking her?"

"No."

"Was she on the pill?"

"No."

"Anything?"

"Not to my knowledge."

"Well what in the hell did you think would happen when you're fucking her raw?"

Gabe gave a chuckle before getting up to grab a Corona from the bar. Mr. Williams was always straight no chaser so his vernacular didn't surprise me.

"To be honest, I wasn't thinking about that—"

"Obviously."

"No disrespect, Mr. Williams, but what's done is done and I'm not trying to change it or make any excuses for it. I hate like hell that Stephanie and I have reached this point in our marriage. Hell, sometimes I sit and try to figure out how we got here. You know I loved the shit out of Stephanie, would have given anything to make her happy, but . . . shit happens . . . people change. And Stephanie and I did a hell of a whole lot of changing, and as you can see Mr. Williams, we haven't changed for the best."

He rubbed his chin and picked his cigar back up before continuing, "I hear what you're saying but don't bullshit me Aric. You still want to be with my baby girl, or not?"

As he talked he moved his hand around and the cigar flicked between his fingers. His eyes were directly on me and I removed my glasses before I answered. Gabe had casually removed himself from the conversation and was leaning on the bar with a beer in his hand looking on.

"I've been asking Stephanie for a divorce for the past two years almost, Mr. Williams. Two years," I repeated holding up the same amount of fingers to get my point across. "We've been having—"

"Two years, huh?" he interrupted.

Mr. Williams was that kind of guy. Although he listened to everything being said, he pulled out parts that were most important to him.

"Two years," I repeated.

He moved around on his stool before puffing his cigar and putting it back down on the ash tray. "I see there's a lot going on that I don't know about. So just what in the hell is going on with you two Aric? How do two people who've been together for as long as you and Stephanie get to this point? It wouldn't make sense to throw all of that time invested away at this point would it? You guys have been through hell and back together."

"I don't think there's any more good we could do for one another at this point. Too much has happened . . ."

"Cecilia and I have been together for over forty years, since she was sixteen. I've put that woman through shit that I can't even imagine enduring. Had a son with her best friend"—he nodded toward Gabe as he mentioned that last part—"cheated on her countless times, fought with her, put my hands on her in ways a man should never touch a woman, especially not his woman, and she still stuck with me. Now, I know my baby girl. She is every bit of her mother so I know you have had to deal with a bunch of bullshit, but to walk away from it all? What would be the point in wasting all of that time?"

"I see it one way Mr. Williams and you see it another. I still love her enough to let her go. I still love her enough to allow her a chance at being happy again because staying with me is not going to make her happy. I don't . . . want to be in this marriage anymore. I'm tired of arguing, tired of fighting, tired of us cheating on one another, fighting about that, making up, and repeating the cycle all over again. I'm to the point that I just want peace Mr. Williams. All I want is peace and where Stephanie and I are right now, we will never have peace with one another. Never."

I had been talking with my hands, mad that my sentiment about the subject was getting to me. Mr. Williams didn't say anything for a few minutes as he looked like he was deep in thought. My phone started vibrating on the table and I knew it was Chyanne without looking at it.

"And you say it has nothing to do with . . . this—this . . . girl—"

"Chyanne."

"Chyanne. Your feelings have nothing to do with her?"

"No."

"How old is this girl?"

"Twenty-five."

Gabe tossed me a beer. I caught it mid-air and nodded my thanks to him. He offered one to his father, but he declined.

Mr. Williams blew out steam, shook his head, and looked at me again. "You're fucking a twenty-five year old? Got her pregnant? You didn't think that this would bother your wife, Aric? The woman who has been trying to have a baby by you for a while now?"

I frowned my face and looked at him after taking a huge gulp of beer. "Mr. Williams, Stephanie aborted our last child together. If she was trying to have my baby, she could have fooled me with that one."

By the way he looked at me I could tell that was news to him. He slowly leaned on the table and clasped his big hands together. To any lesser man, the way Mr. Williams was looking at me would have intimidated them. My phone vibrated again and again I ignored it. Mr. Williams scratched his head before looking over at me again.

"Son, what I'm trying to convey to you here is that even with all you've just told me, what you and Stephanie have endured should have—"

"Mr. Williams, would you want me to stay with your daughter if you knew that we've physically fought with one another? If you knew that I've had to physically put my hands on her to sometimes get my point across, would you still want me to be with her?"

I knew I was taking a huge risk. The one thing Mr. Williams did not play about was any man putting his hands on his daughter. He could have jumped across the table and tried to put his foot in my ass. I actually believe he was contemplating it with the way he was rubbing his hands together staring at me. I knew my words stung him, pulled at the love he had in heart for Stephanie. I'd said it in a way that my words would have that effect. The one thing I hated was for a person to tell me how to run my life. No matter who the hell it was. Nobody was going to force me to stay somewhere I wasn't happy. No one was going to tell me I didn't have the right to live my life the way I wanted to and although I knew Mr. Williams could still kick ass like the best prized fighter, an ass whooping is what I would not take—from any man.

So as he leaned back in his chair and sat upright as if his spine would break if someone pushed him the wrong way, I knew he was either going to respect what I was saying or jump up and test my manhood. We never got a chance to test my theory. The door to the basement flew open and Stephanie came barging down the stairs. The look on her face led me to believe that she had been eavesdropping on what her father and I been discussing. I was wrong however. As her mother stood at the top of the stairs with her with both hands on her hips looking as if she was staring at a ghost, Chyanne rounded the corner. I didn't know whether to be mad, embarrassed, pissed, or downright surprised. I knew Chyanne didn't like confrontation so for her to be in my house meant she must have had something really important to say to me.

I watched as she slowly made her way down the stairs. I could see on her face that she hadn't expected for me to have a full house and even though it was a very tense situation for us all, her beauty was still not lost on me. Her hair was pulled back into a sleek pony tail allowing that pregnancy glow to enhance her beauty. She wore no makeup and the chocolate lip gloss reminded me of how lush and soft her lips were. Pregnancy was supposed to make you gain weight, but it looked as if Chyanne had dropped a few pounds. She had on the black leather jacket I had bought her, a pair of light denim jeans fit snug against her legs and thighs, a button down white shirt flared over her full belly and hips, and a pair of black boots were on her feet. I could tell she had taken extra care in her appearance for this occasion.

Her chocolate eyes took in the scene around her. She was a smart woman so it wasn't that hard for her to figure out that she was in the presence of Stephanie's parents. There was a manila envelope in her hand and my heart rate increased. I had been so caught up in what was going on that the paternity test had completely slipped my mind.

"Hi," Chyanne spoke when she stood beside me at the table.

"Hello, young lady," Mr. Williams replied.

"I didn't know Aric had company or I wouldn't have come, but I just needed to drop something off to him."

I had no idea why she felt the need to be explaining herself. That annoyed me, but before I could speak up Stephanie blurted out, "You could have called."

She'd taken up a defensive stance next to her father. Her arms were folded and I knew it still grated her nerves that Chyanne had gotten the best of her in their fight. All I could think about, however, was the envelope in Chyanne's hand and what the contents inside would mean for me.

"I did call. In fact, I've called several times."

I finally looked up to see that Chyanne and Stephanie were in a stare down and when Mrs. Williams came to stand beside her daughter and husband, I figured we needed to get whatever Chyanne had to say to me out of the way.

"What's up Chyanne," Gabe spoke from behind her.

She turned and a slow easy smile brightened her face at the sight of Gabe. My nerves got jittery and for some reason the shit annoyed me too.

"Hi, Gabe. How are you?"

"Couldn't be better," he replied as he casually stood upright and gave her a once over.

"What do you want?" I asked bringing her attention back to me.

She looked offended as she dropped the envelope on the table before me. It seemed as if all eyes were on me except for Stephanie's. Her eyes were on the manila envelope Chyanne had just dropped on the table.

"What is that?" I asked although I knew what it was.

"Test results."

"What do they say?"

"I don't know. I didn't look."

I could tell she was nervous by the way she was looking at me. The whole room was silent and although I wished I could have read the results in private, I knew to ask anyone in the room other than Gabe to leave would be a problem. I looked across the table and Stephanie already had tears in her eyes. When she noticed I was looking at her she shook her head and wiped the tears away.

"This is such bullshit," she said in a low tone but loud enough to be heard by us all.

"It'll all work itself out," her mother said to her while her hand moved up and down Stephanie's back trying to relax her.

Chyanne kept her eyes on me when she spoke. "I can leave."

"You shouldn't have even come! Disrespectful bitch," Stephanie shouted at her.

"Stephanie calm down," her father said to her.

"No! No, I shouldn't have to calm down. This is my damn house and I shouldn't have to be disrespected like this by my husband's whore."

She was irate and her fists were balled at her side. I didn't know what it felt like to be in her shoes, but I can't say that I was happy about putting her in this position. In the same breath, the need to know if Chyanne was carrying my child was eating away at me. I'd never even known I wanted to be a father as bad as I did until that envelope was in front of me.

"The only reason I'm not saying anything to you right now is because I'm assuming these are your parents and I'm trying to remain as respectful as I can in this situation," Chyanne stated.

"I think you passed the grounds of respect when you slept with a married man," Mrs. Williams told Chyanne.

"Then you both will have to take that up with Aric since I had no idea he was married until his wife attacked me."

In that moment I realized I had to take control of the situation before it got out of hand. I pulled myself away from my thoughts long enough to take a hold of Chyanne's wrist to keep her from leaving. I wanted her to be right there when I opened the envelope. Mr. Williams leaned forward and cleared his throat as I quickly opened the envelope and removed its contents. I read through all of the rhetoric and got to the part that I needed to see.

"*. . . all of the genetic loci has been tested. The mother's sample has been included in the DNA testing and the percentage probability that the tested father is 99.999% of a match. The tested father cannot be excluded as the tested child's biological father . . .*"

I didn't know what I felt at that moment as a sudden wave of anxiety overtook me. I kept reading that same passage over and over just so I could make sure I was reading it correctly. I looked over at Chyanne and her look said 'I told you so'. I wanted to reach out and hug her but knew that would cause a reaction that I wouldn't want. Laying the papers back on the table I allowed Mr. Williams to pick them up and read it for himself. I looked at the woman who had been my wife for fifteen years and I didn't have to open my mouth and tell her what she already knew. Her pride wouldn't allow her to stay in the same room with the embarrassment, hurt, and anger that I could see on her face. So when she stormed off up the stairs, I knew that she had gotten the answer that she was hoping not to receive. Her mother went after her but not before she told me exactly what a low down dirty bastard she thought I was.

Chyanne

I was nervous, pacing back and forth waiting for Aric to arrive. Finding out he was indeed the father of the child I was carrying was like another heavy burden had been lifted off of me. To say that it hadn't been mind boggling to be in the room with his wife and her parents when he was reading the results would be a lie. I had never been as nervous, scared, and out of place as I was in that moment. I had to stand there and be called all kinds of female dogs and whores and I really had no real way to defend myself. How could I be mad at a woman who had every right to be upset that her husband had cheated on her and got another woman pregnant? How could I be mad at her for feeling the way I probably would have felt regardless of the fact that I didn't know Aric was married? Even still, when I tried to talk to let her know that I did feel some empathy for what she was going through, she still attacked me and my character at every chance she got.

Who knows exactly what she was feeling standing there watching her husband read the results that said he'd fathered my child?

All in all, that didn't stop my love for Aric. It didn't stop me from being anxious to see him and it didn't stop me from missing him. Call me what you want, but being in love with a married man wasn't easy for me, being in love with a man like Aric wasn't easy period. So I guess you could say that I was my mother all over again. All night in my mind, I wracked my brain trying to figure out how I had gotten myself into the mess I was in. Was April correct? Did I fall for the first man who showed a genuine interest in me? Aric had swooped in and swept me completely off my feet and even though, after a while, I knew there was another woman I kept on loving him . . . hoping that one day there would be only me. So I guess I really was one of those stupid women my mother cursed under her breath.

I almost jumped out of my skin when Aric walked through my front door. I hadn't even realized I'd still been standing there until I looked into his face. It was hard to read what he was thinking. Only hours before I'd left his home when his wife and her mother came back in the basement and confronted me. I had to give it to Stephanie she always said what she felt. So when she came storming back down the stairs and got in my face, I was kind of expecting it. Luckily there were three men in the room who were able to diffuse the situation before it got worse. For the most part, I let Stephanie do the talking and the name calling. All I wanted to do was let Aric know that he was my child's father and there was pretty much nothing any of us could do about that.

"Hey," I said breathlessly as he pulled the keys from the door knob and closed the door behind him.

I had no idea what to expect from him. I was just happy to see him just as I was when seeing him earlier.

"Hey, yourself," he greeted before removing his leather jacket and discarding it on my loveseat. "How're you feeling?"

"I don't know. I guess it depends on how you're feeling," I answered nervously as I stuck my hand in the back pocket of my jeans.

"How should I be feeling?"

I shrugged. "I don't know, you tell me. I know I probably caused a lot of trouble earlier . . ."

"No more than would have been caused anyway," he explained as we continued to stare at one another.

It was like that for a while. In that moment, I could tell that things had changed for Aric and me. The fact that I was carrying his baby showed me a softer side of him as we just stood there and stared at one another. He looked from me to my stomach from time to time. You never knew what you would get with Aric. He was very unpredictable. My anxiety intensified as he closed the gap between us.

"So this is my child, huh?" He asked as he reached out to touch my stomach.

I nodded and gave a shy smile. A wave of sudden exhilaration came over me at the feel of his hands on my stomach and when he smiled at me I knew he was happy with the news that he was going to be a father. Moments like that one was when I fell deeper in love with him. I let him unbutton my shirt from the bottom up so he could feel my skin against his hands. Looking at him in that moment showed me a side of him I'd rarely seen . . . the soft, caring, and nurturing side of the man that I'd found myself wanting to be with so badly. In that moment I decided that I would do whatever it took to keep him in my life. Married or not, I needed him. I needed him to help me with his child and I needed him for my sanity.

I don't know how to explain what I felt when he slowly pulled layer after layer of my clothes away and led me to my bedroom. He made love to me that day like we had never done before. Aric was an aggressive lover, but not this time. No. He took his time and placed kisses on every inch of my body, but when he took the time to gently place kisses on my stomach and talk to our child, that's what stood out to me the most. And when he finally connected his body to mine, I knew that he would always have me right where he wanted me.

It was a little after seven in the evening and Aric was helping me to clean out my spare bedroom since that would be where the baby's domain would be. Although I was happy with him being there and glad that we were getting along, I needed to convince him to give me my job back. Having a job meant having security for my child and that was important to me.

"Can I talk to you for a minute?" I asked him standing in the door way watching him as he moved boxes of stuff around the room.

"Go ahead."

He stood from the crouching position he was in and looked at me as I walked into the room and sat on a box that was in the far right corner. His hands were dirty and he had worked up a sweat. He wasn't wearing his glasses so at times he narrowed his eyes to get a better look at me.

"I wanted to talk to you about getting my job back. I mean, I have money saved up, but I would feel better knowing I had income coming in with the baby on the way."

He folded one arm under the other and rubbed his bald head before answering. He shook his head and answered, "No."

I was shocked. I can't lie. I wasn't expecting him to come right out and say no. "Really? Why?"

"Because it wouldn't be in either of our best interest."

"What am I supposed to do about a job?"

"Look for another one."

"In this economy I wouldn't even find a job that would hire me, let alone find one that would hire me while I'm pregnant," I argued. "Look, I wouldn't even have to work for you. Maybe you could switch assistants with someone else—"

"Hell no," he fumed. "You coming back to the office would not be good. Too much talking about us is still going on . . ."

"So you're worried about what people will think?"

"No," he said as he went back to moving boxes around. "I'm worried about how it would look if I was checking on you every hour on the hour. People would know something was going on and it wouldn't be long before they figured out that it's my child you're carrying."

"So what? I need a job Aric!"

He put the box down that he was holding and looked at me. "Two things; that tone in your voice, get rid of it. This shit isn't easy for me either Chyanne, so stop making it all about you! You know damn well you don't have to worry about money. I can take care of you and my child."

"This isn't about you taking care of me Aric," I said as I felt myself get annoyed. "I don't need you to take care of me. I'm perfectly capable of taking care of myself, however; having stable income for my child would make me feel better."

He exhaled gave me a look that told me I was annoying him. "You're not getting your job back and that's that. Take that however you want it, but I'm not about to have the board breathing down my neck and I'm sure as hell not about to be dealing with my wife . . ."

Before he could finish that last sentence, I got up and stormed out of the room. Nobody asked him about his damned wife.

"Chyanne."

He called me two more times and I ignored him. Mentioning her the way he did pissed me off. I was angry and angrier than I had been in a long time. I slammed my door in anger and for a quick second forgetting about the man I was dealing with, forgetting that my attitude, tone of voice, and slamming the door was a sure fire way to set him off. He quickly reminded me of just who the hell he was when he shoved my bedroom open so hard that it felt as if the room shook. Infuriation and anger were written all over his face. I quickly sat down on the bed because I didn't know what else to do, but he snatched me up by my wrist and pulled me close to him. He used his free hand to make me look up at him. Although the grip he had on my chin wasn't hard enough to hurt me, it was firm enough to let me know that he meant business.

"Why are you showing your ass right now? You know damn well if I could give you your job back I would. Think about this shit for a second baby . . . would it be worth the headache or the stress it would cause you to have to deal with her? And you know she would make both of our lives a living hell. You want me to lose my job? Huh? You want me to not be able to help you with this baby? Come on baby, work with me. I'm trying to do what's best for everybody, but if you're going to start showing your ass on me then we, you and me, will have a problem. Understand?"

I didn't respond as I looked up into his eyes, but he continued, "I know this isn't going to be easy, but we don't have to make it any harder."

As he finished he let go of my face and I sat back down on my bed with my arms folded across my chest still upset that he cared more about how his wife would feel than about me being able to take care of his child.

"Look, I'll make a few phone calls and see if I can get you in somewhere else," he said when he saw I really didn't want to buy what he was selling. "That's the best I can do baby."

He said that with a take it or leave it attitude before leaving me to my own resources. I stayed in my room away from him and allowed him to finish what he was doing in the room. We didn't say too much to each other unless he asked me if I wanted to keep something or when I took him food and something to drink. Several times his phone rang and each time I knew it was his wife because I could hear him going off on her. I was half asleep, and half watching the Being Human marathon on Syfy channel by the time he finished.

"I guess you've forgotten about this?" He asked me.

I sat up and looked at what he was referring to. When I'd found out he was married and he'd shown up at my house, I was so hurt and angered by the news that I took the ring off and threw it at his face. In his hand he held the ring he'd place on my finger on my birthday and to be honest I had forgotten about it. But, I hadn't forgotten about the events that took place that same day he'd given it to me and a few days after.

I smiled and looked into his smiling face. "Where'd you find it?"

"When I was cleaning the room it tumbled from underneath the door."

I guess when I threw it and it bounced into the hall it rolled under the door in my spare bedroom.

He chuckled. "That was the first time I'd ever heard you curse. You tossed that shit at my head and called me a lying son of a bitch. Remember that?"

I nodded. "I was mad. I rarely curse, but when I do it's with reason."

He smiled and nodded before his expression turned serious and he looked at me. "It's a lot of shit I need to apologize to you for, but I have this thing with apologizing for things that I feel won't do you any good to hear. So, will you put this back on your finger for me if I promise that the shit that has gone down with us before won't ever happen again?"

I wanted to let my emotions overtake me because it was rare that I got to see or hear Aric express any emotion to me, but I kept my feelings at bay. I looked into his eyes and wondered just what this moment was going to mean for us. I wanted to hear him say he loved me. I wanted to hear him say he cared for me again. I wanted so much from him that I knew would be impossible to get with him still being married so I took what I could get. That's why I nodded and let him slide the ring back on my finger. I loved this man and the love I had for him would be my undoing if I didn't get control of it and soon.

When he kneeled down to kiss me goodnight, he made it a long passionate kiss that sent me reeling.

"I'll come back in the morning and we can talk about how you want to set up everything in the room. If you want I'll pick up the crib and whatever else you figure you want and need or we could shop for that stuff together. Just let me know what you want to do, alright?

I nodded again feeling overjoyed at the prospect of spending more time with him even if it was only about the baby. When he kissed me again, this time just a passionate peck on the lips, my heart melted and I was putty in his hands all over again. *What the heck are you doing*, I asked myself after he had gone and I'd laid back down on the couch. Are you really about to be the glorified *'other woman'*?

I lay there on my couch for a while asking myself the same question over and over until I made myself get up and look at the job he had done in the guest room. The marks from the vacuum were fresh on the carpet and the room smelled of apple cinnamon carpet powder. It was a total transformation. The full sized bed had been placed by the big bay window and made up with a red, white, and black comforter set that had been in the closet. Boxes had been sorted and what wasn't thrown away had been taken to the garage, except for the few I wanted to keep in the house. Now that the room was clean, I could see just how big it was. There was a lot of space that I would need as time progressed. I smiled to myself and was about to turn the light out and leave the room until a picture of my parents on the wood grain bookcase caught my eye.

I knew he'd found that picture in one of the many boxes and it was like looking at ghosts as I stared at the two people I looked so much alike. I slowly picked up the picture and it was like I was looking at them for the first time. There they stood. My mom had the biggest smile on her face that I had ever seen. I can't remember if I ever saw her smile that lively when I was a kid. My dad had her wrapped in a hug so tight it was as if they were melted together and the smile on his face was just as vibrant and alive as hers. The picture had been taken at what looked to be a family function, because I could make out other family members in the background. You wouldn't be able to look at that picture and see the pain, anger, and violence that plagued our house. My mom was my height . . . cute in the face, thick in the breast and hips, and very small in the waist. She had a body that would make any woman grab her man closer. Her wild mane reminded me of the fro I once had just a few months ago and made me absentmindedly run my fingers through my hair. People always told me we looked identical. I looked at my dad as tears fell down my face. I wish I would have known my parents when they were in that place in time before images of my father's hand connecting with my mother's face haunted me.

After a while I was finally able to pull myself together and prepare for bed. The fact that I didn't have a job or a job prospect still bothered me until I remembered Shelley's card in my purse. I looked at the clock and it was a little after one in the morning. I didn't expect her to answer, but I picked up my phone, grabbed her card, and dialed her number.

"This is Shelley," she answered.

"Hey. I know it's late—"

"Chyanne! Please tell me you're calling to tell me you're all in," she exclaimed. "I'm at my wits end and could really use you girl!"

"What comes with the "all in" title?" I asked her.

"Are you busy right now?"

"No, not really. Why?"

"Can I meet you or you meet me at an IHOP or something? I'll bring everything needed. I want to talk to you about being my partner actually . . ."

As she talked, I thought to myself that I wasn't expecting anything more than an executive assistant's position or at least another position in the company, but not a partner. What did I have to lose, though? I had no job and didn't think I had a great chance of finding one at the moment. I threw on something comfortable, grabbed my resume, and made my way to meet Shelley.

Aric

Gabe and I had been working so long and so hard on the merger that I knew I'd damn near run myself into the ground. Early days and late nights was what it had been for the last past three weeks. I was focused more than ever and besides wanting to make sure the merger of two of the biggest firms in the region debuted strong, I also needed to get away from Stephanie. She had been on a hell storm and I had not been in the mood to deal with it. I'd probably made things worse by spending as much time with Chyanne as I had been, but when a man had the task of choosing between peace and bullshit, my money would bet he'd choose peace.

Not only that, but Chyanne and I had been busy getting things prepared for the baby. She and I had gone shopping for little things she'd felt she would need. Some of the stuff I didn't understand why she would need it, like the breast pump. If she was going to breast feed then why buy a pump when the baby would be latched on to her titty? We'd also gone to my personal bank so I could set up an account to put money in for the baby. Although I trusted Chyanne to do what she was supposed to do for my child, I still wanted an itemized account of everything.

With all that Chyanne and I had been doing to prepare for the baby, and all the time that I'd been spending with her, all Stephanie's mind could think of was me having sex with Chyanne. And yes, quite a few times, I'd indulged myself between her thighs, but all of our time was not spent having sex. I knew that what Stephanie had been dealing with had to be mentally draining, but I still didn't think it was an excuse for her to carry on the way she had been. She'd become angry and bitter and I'll admit to my fault in that, but it was nothing new for Stephanie. Throughout our marriage she'd had spells where she would be purely evil because she felt like it most times, but I was so excited about being a father that nothing else mattered. The feeling that I'd get watching Chyanne's stomach grow with my child was overwhelming at times. I would find myself laying my head on her lap while we'd be watching TV just so I could find a way to be closer to the baby.

"Aric," Gabe called out to me.

We'd been doing some number crunching that needed both of our full attention, especially because we'd decided to do it head on. When dealing with budget proposals and trying to merge companies' assets it was a very complex and lengthy process and my head was all over the place.

"Yeah," I answered knowing his reason for calling me.

"That's the fifth damn time I've told you that equation won't work and you keep putting that shit down. Get your head back in the game or go take a break."

He was annoyed and he had a right to be. We both needed to be paying close attention to detail in what we were doing on the spreadsheets and I wasn't.

"We've been at this shit since six this morning," I said to him looking at the Cartier watch on my arm. "It's damn near two and I need to eat anyway."

I was annoyed with my damn self. I'd sat with Chyanne the night before because she'd been sick. That caused another fight between Stephanie and me. No

matter how many times I'd said I wasn't fucking Chyanne but was there because she was sick, she heard and
believed what she wanted.

"What's on your mind anyway?" he asked as he took
a seat in the chair behind him.

We'd been in my office because we didn't want to
be bothered and being in the boardroom would have
meant the possibility of being interrupted.

"Didn't get much sleep," I said covering my mouth to
stifle a yawn before continuing. "Chyanne being sick all
the time is not allowing me to get much rest."

"Something wrong with the baby?"

I shook my head. "Doctor says the baby is fine. She's
just one of those women who stay sick the whole pregnancy I guess. Had to put up with Stephanie's bullshit
too."

I went to the hidden liquor cabinet behind the office
bookshelf and pulled out a bottle of Hennessey Ellipse
and some Louis XIII Black Pearl Limited Edition co-
gnac. The Ellipse would get me a fast steady buzz, but
the Black Pearl would sneak up on me so I decided to
go with that one. I needed something that would mel-
low my ass out and help me to relax. After ordering
lunch from PF Chang's and pouring both Gabe and
myself a glass, I sat down in my desk chair and let my
head fall back as the Black Pearl molested my tongue
going down.

"I take it you had to stay with Chyanne last night and
Stephanie didn't like that too much?" Gabe inquired.

I sat up and put my empty glass on the desk. "She
showed her ass and she showed up at Chyanne's
house."

"What? Get the fuck outta here!"

His voice clearly showed that he was amused and
shocked. Those deep baritones laugh of his resonated
around the office.

I chuckled. "That shit ain't funny, Gabe."

"Like hell! You can't tell me that you believed you would ever see the day Stephanie would do some shit like that. I don't know man . . . Chyanne must have gotten under her skin about you and her."

"I don't know, but as soon as I saw that red Mercedes pull up I was out the door and I put a stop to that before it even started."

"I wonder how she found out where Chy lived, though . . ."

"You know Stephanie, probably sweet talked one of your father's FBI friends."

"Oh yeah, you're probably right, but damn," he laughed again. "You and Chy together has Stephanie all bent out of shape." He knocked his drink back and placed the empty glass on my desk before pouring another one and returning to sit on the couch.

To think about what he'd said, he was right. I don't ever remember Stephanie going as far before as she was doing with Chyanne. "I don't know why though. I keep telling her that me not wanting to be with her has nothing to do with Chyanne."

"Yeah, but . . . are you sure about that?" He asked as he sat back and cast a skeptical look my direction.

I frowned. "What the hell do you mean am I sure?"

"Just what I asked, are you sure?"

"Come on Gabe. You of all people should know how long I've been asking for a fucking divorce!"

"I do and I know, but . . . I don't know. I guess I see something else when I see you and Chyanne together. Say what you want, there is something about that full figured chocolate woman that gets you all bent out of shape."

I looked at him like he had lost his mind as I walked around to the front of my desk and leaned on it with my arms folded. "Bent out of shape?" I repeated as if I hadn't really heard him when he said it the first time.

He laughed. "Come on Aric. We've been boys for how long? I know you enough to know that your feelings are running a little deeper for Chy than you are putting on."

"I care a lot about her because she's the mother—"

"You cared about her before then!"

"I did, but not on the level you're insinuating."

"Bullshit, Aric! Real bullshit! Get the fuck outta here. You say that shit now, but let another motherfucker try to get at her and all hell is going to break loose," he said and laughed.

We both laughed. "Kiss my ass Gabe. You can't tell me how I feel about someone—"

"You're right, but I can tell you what I see and I see that Chy has an effect on you whether you want to admit it or not. Stephanie sees it and it's fucking with her mentally I bet. And if she doesn't see what Chy does to you . . . she's seeing what you do to Chy."

On one hand I was laughing at his *repartee* and on the other he was seriously annoying me with trying to tell me what was going on between Chyanne and me.

"The girl loves you and you know it," he continued.

I nodded because he was correct.

"My thing is, why make her fall in love with you and you know you don't even want to be with her like that?"

I pulled the sleeves up on the red V-neck sweater I was wearing. "I didn't make her fall in love with me."

"You know what I mean Aric. You got that girl so caught up in you that she stood there and let Stephanie and her mother call her all kinds of names and all she did was look at you from time to time to gauge your reaction. That girl would do anything for you and you know it. She may hate loving you, but she loves you all the same."

Before I could go off on him like I'd had a good mind to do at that moment, because he had pissed me the fuck off in his assessment of me 'making' Chyanne love me, April pushed my office door open and walked in like she owned something in there. We both looked at her with surprise. It had been a little chilly when I left for work that morning, but judging by how short her denim skirt was I could safely assume it had warmed up. Looking at her dressed the way she was at thirty-five and a mother of three teenage boys reminded me of why I fucked her once and forgot about her. She had been calling me over the last few weeks and I'd been ignoring most of her calls because, really, we had nothing to talk about. Having sex with her hadn't been that serious for me.

She smiled at me first and then Gabe before speaking. "Hello, you two! How's it been?"

Anybody who'd known me knew the one thing I hated was for someone to barge into my office unannounced and without an appointment. Instead of returning her greeting like Gabe had done, I allowed my silence to speak for me.

"Hello Aric," she greeted and tried to hug me.

I brushed her off and walked around to sit behind my desk. Don't get me wrong she was a beautiful woman with her butterscotch tan skin and her body was the stuff most men dreamed about. I just wasn't as impressed as I had been before I'd fucked her.

"What's up April?" I asked after I'd sat back casually in my chair and looked up at her.

She stood there with a surprised look on her face as if she was expecting a different reception.

"So, I can't get a hug?"

I sighed loudly. "We were in the middle of some very important work. Is there anything we could help you with?"

April struck me as the vengeful and vindictive kind of woman; the kind of woman that plotted your downfall, all the while smiling in your face. Any woman who would fuck a man just to make her friend mad, really couldn't do shit for me. I never really liked her to begin with, but since she was throwing pussy around and her body made my dick curious, I obliged myself inside of her. Her head game was immaculate; the stuff super head legends were made of.

"Well could you make time, a minute or two, for an old friend?" She asked with a hopeful and flirtatious smile on her face.

Gabe chuckled and threw his head back in amusement.

I looked at my watch. "Your two minutes start now," I said to her.

She huffed and gave an ersatz chuckle. "Any particular reason you're in my office April?" I asked her after I saw she was just wasting my time.

"I came to talk to you about something Chyanne told me and I just came by to say hi."

As she talked she moved her neck and it was clear that the chipper mood she'd walked in the door with was gone.

"Well you've said hi. Now what else can I help you with?"

"Are you really married and if so why didn't you tell me before we had sex? I don't sleep with married men."

When Gabe laughed out loud, I couldn't help but to chuckle myself. "Let me get this right"—I started as I leaned on my desk and clasped my hands together before me staring at her with a bemused expression— "you're telling me that my having a wife bothers you more than letting me fuck you just to make your 'best friend' mad?"

I remembered she had told me that after the one time that we'd had sex. Afterwards she proceeded to tell me she was glad she'd done it because the sex was good . . . too bad I couldn't tell her the same.

"If I would have known you were married, I wouldn't have had sex with you at all!" She had the nerve to have attitude in her voice. "Having sex with married men is not something I do."

"But betraying the woman who was supposed to be your closest friend is?"

"That really has nothing to do with you. That's between me and Chyanne—"

"That's what you came down here to tell me? You could have called and left a message."

I was intentionally being an asshole and I knew it. So did Gabe which was probably why he'd been shaking his head and getting a kick out of it. I didn't know why she thought she could just show up at my office and expect the reaction to be other that what she'd gotten besides I still remembered that shady shit she pulled on Chyanne when we all were at that business social.

"You know what? Fuck you Aric," she snapped and turned to leave. "Fuck you and Chyanne. You two deserve each other."

I stood and moved back around to the front of my desk. "Sorry, but I don't think she rolls that way, but maybe if you saw her in action you could learn a thing or two."

The smirk on my face had to be sinister as she gave me the middle finger and slammed my office door on her way out. Gabe and I made it no secret that we'd both fucked her and the general consensus was the same, her head game was better than the sex.

It wasn't long after that little fiasco that the food we'd ordered was delivered. We ate lunch, and finished up the spreadsheets afterwards. Food and a couple drinks were just what the doctor had ordered, and while I'd been hoping to go home and try to get some sleep in, Stephanie had other plans. She wanted to talk and in order for me to have some semblance of peace I knew I had to do it. So against my better judgment, I'd agreed.

After I'd worked out, showered, changed into some sweats, relaxed a bit, and had been watching the Lakers eat the Hawks alive, she came into the living room to start my interrogation. I watched her as she briskly walked into the front room while her pony tail swung from side to side like a pendulum. She sat on the end of the couch opposite me and tucked her long lithe legs under her. Although I turned the TV off, I didn't move from my laid-back position on the couch. There was a brief moment of silence where we both just gazed at each other. I could tell she had been crying. I saw no tears, but the puffiness around her eyes gave it away as well as the balled up tissue in her hand.

"Do you love me Aric?" She asked suddenly.

I closed my eyes briefly and exhaled. I'd known she would start off with that question. "I will always love you Stephanie," I said looking at her as she slowly blinked. "There's no way you can go through what we have and I not love you."

"But you're no longer in love with me?"

"Stephanie, why do we keep doing this same dance over and over?"

"Because you're never straight forward with me Aric. You evade questions, answer questions with a question, and I never really know just what the hell you're thinking. I need some answers Aric. That's all I'm asking."

I finally sat up. "What answers Stephanie? Everything you ask, I tell you."

She started shaking her head. "No you don't Aric, you don't."

Her tears had started to fall and the one thing I could not deal with was her crying. I'd begun to get annoyed, but because I really didn't want to fight with her I continued to talk.

"What do you want to know that I haven't told you yet Stephanie?" I asked using the back of one hand slapping it in the palm of the other.

"Why her?" She asked after a moment of silence.

I wasn't quite sure I understood her question. "Why, who? What do you mean, why her?"

"Why Chyanne? What is it about her that made you want to get her pregnant?"

I sighed loudly. "See, that's the problem, no matter what I tell you, you will hear what you want to hear. I've told you that it wasn't planned . . ."

"You can say that all you want, but the fact that you didn't use a condom with her tells me a lot. I know you Aric. I know the fucking man I've been with for twenty damn years! I know how you are about STD's and HIV, so she must be something special if you were fucking her without a condom. So what is it about her?"

I shook my head and chuckled lightly in my irritation. "You can laugh all you want, but—"

"There is no but, Stephanie. I didn't plan to get her pregnant!"

"But you didn't do anything to prevent it either! You had her in this house, our home!"

"This house"—I said standing and pointing to the floor as I spoke—"this house, my money bought. So this is my house."

"And I'm your wife," she said defensively as she jumped up from the couch. "What's yours will always be mine! The fact of the matter is, you had her in the very house that we have sex in. I have to lie in the bed that you've probably had sex with her in and, since it's you we're talking about, I know you've fucked her in this house." Her right fist had been balled around the wad of tissue in her hand while she used the left to move around to get her point across. "All through the holidays we talked Aric. We were talking about making our marriage work and then all of a sudden . . . nothing! Just like that? If your decision has nothing to do with her then let me know exactly what the hell is going on."

"Damn it! For the last . . . fucking . . . time, Chyanne has nothing to do with me wanting a divorce!" I stepped closer to her and held my hands in front of me as if I was praying because God knows in that moment it was taking all that was within me to remain sane and calm. "You know just as well as I do that this shit we call a marriage is nothing more than a façade at this point. It's all a show. How many times must we cheat, fight, curse, and fuss before we say enough is enough? Twenty years Stephanie, and I swear it feels like for the last ten all we've done was build each other up and violently tear each other back down. Why must we go on baby? Is it worth it?"

"It's worth it to me Aric, because I'm still in love with the man I met twenty years ago. I'm still in love with my husband," she cried and it hurt like hell to see her look as if she was breaking under the pressure as she spoke through bated breaths. "No matter what I've done or what I've said I've never, not once, stopped loving you. I can be woman enough right now to say, I've done things and said things to you that I knew would hurt, but that was because I was immature back then. I wasn't able to handle a man like you loving me. I watched you change Aric. I watched you go from who you were at nineteen to who you are now and I know I had a hand in that. I never once doubted you loved me then, but it hurts . . ." she said as her words got stuck in the swell of her throat. I reached out to pull her into my arms and she shook her head.

"I need to say this. It hurts like hell to watch the way you look at Chyanne because I know you looked at me the same way once. Whether you care to admit it or not Aric, the feelings you have for her are visible and it hurts to know that I had a hand in turning our relationship into what it is. I'm so angry at myself because I used the things you told me about your mother and your childhood to hurt you . . ."

She tried to keep talking but her emotions took over and we both stood there in silence letting our unspoken words speak for us.

It was the first time in a long time that Stephanie had opened up to me the way she'd done, and even though I felt every emotion and truth in what she was saying, I was to the point of no return. I guess I was one of those men who would never understand women. The only difference between me and Stephanie at that moment was that she knew my dirt, it was out in the open. But, while she stood there and told me how much she loved me, all I could think about was how many men she'd cheated on me with. There was once she got so bold as to come home with the smell of one still on her. There were a lot of things a man could deal with, but smelling another man's sex on your wife wasn't one of them.

All of the shit she said about using what I'd told her about the things my mother would say and do to me as a child, that was a big factor in the deterioration of our marriage. I've never talked about my mother because dealing with the pain from that was something I'd have to deal with later. I've never had disdain for any woman the way I had contempt for my mother. Before anybody decides to judge me for my thoughts about her, I loved her, but my father walking out on her seemed to turn her into this angry bitter woman. I guess the only way to feel she was getting back at him was to humiliate me for fun. What she thought was discipline any fool would have known it was downright abuse. If the slaps across my face and head weren't enough then her verbal abuse took the cake. I think I would have favored the physical slaps, the hits with the iron, the broom, and the broken wooden bat across my shoulder over the shit that woman used to say to me. I rarely spoke to my mother and when I did it was brief.

After over fifteen years of being apart and living separately my mother and my father decided to get back together. I can say that my mother had changed. She was a different woman than she was back then and until about five years ago my father and I didn't have the best relationship. As a kid when your parents split and daddy walks out, he's automatically seen as the bad guy. Not to say that my father wasn't around when I was growing up, but for me living in that house alone with my mother, he wasn't around enough. He told me a while back that he just wanted to avoid my mother as much as he possibly could back then. They had a very antagonistic and volatile relationship so my father made the decision to leave. That never sat well with my mother, but he said he did what he thought was best for me. He told me he had seen what was going on between him and my mother when he was a kid and that he didn't want that for me. Little did he know that I would have taken seeing them fight and come out better than living with my mother alone. They both had their side of the story, but when I was a kid the only side that should have mattered was mine.

Stephanie and I stood in the middle of the front room, locked in a battle of wills. Sometimes we'd yell, other times we watched each other in a cold silent anger. No matter what I said to her to bring some peace of mind or understanding, she would always come up with some excuse to think the worst. So I got tired of talking and returned to my silent angry brooding. Of course she couldn't have that and that was when she went from telling me how much she loved me, to telling me how much she hated me for what I'd done and how much she wished the baby Chayanne carried would die.

My mind couldn't take that; something fragile in me snapped and hit me hard. That would make the second time she'd made some sort of threat against my child and flashes of me snapping and beating her ass crossed my mind. Of course, if I went there, it would be what she wanted. So there we stood, silently fighting.

After our supposed talk didn't end the way she wanted, she went back to her usual old self and I was out of the door, done with the drama.

Chyanne

I was awakened by Aric crawling into the bed with me. Because of the deep sleep I was in it took me a minute to realize what was going on.

"Aric," I called out to him as I tried to turn and look at him.

"Yeah. Go back to sleep," he said as he removed his glasses, placing them on the night stand behind him and getting more comfortable.

Of course my mind was going a mile a minute trying to figure out what would make him leave his home in the middle of the night and come to mine.

"You okay?" I asked once he'd wrapped his arms around me and laid his head behind mine.

"Yes. Go back to sleep."

I could tell he was trying to brush me off and didn't want to talk about whatever it was that was bothering him.

"Are you sure?"

"Yes, Chyanne. Now go back to sleep."

I closed my eyes, but my mind was wide open. Call it what you want, but the enthusiasm in my heart had me floating. As he rubbed my stomach, I smiled to myself. I'd needed his touch and not in a sexual way. I just needed some affection. I hadn't heard from him all day and I'd been wondering if he'd been mad at me so to have had him in my bed brightened my night. His warm solid body nestled next to mine was like soft music to my ears. He'd pulled his clothes off and I could feel him semi-hardened against my backside.

"Did you eat? Do you want me to go fix you something?" I asked because I knew he liked to eat and would get hungry at crazy times.

He chuckled before answering. "Chyanne?"

"Yes."

"Take your ass back to sleep!" I smiled when he kissed the back of my neck.

The rest of the night was a peaceful one. Often throughout the night I would wake up to change positions in bed because being pregnant I found it hard to get comfortable easily. Sometimes I would find him awake staring off into space, other times his eyes would be closed as if he was sleeping. Lying in Aric's arm made it a little less stressful and it wasn't long before I turned to Aric and placed my lips against his. I could tell he was tired, but I'd missed his touch and needed to feel him inside of me. He returned the favor and before leaving for work he gave me what I needed.

Almost a month later, Shelley and I had everything needed in order to get the doors to Johnson & Saxton open. We decided against using the words marketing and advertising after it because it was cliché to us both. The night I'd met Shelley at the IHOP on 85 in Riverdale was the night I decided to take my future into my own hands. Aric wasn't going to give me my job back and although he'd said he would make a few calls on my behalf, I knew he didn't want me to work while I was pregnant. When both my parents had left me, one of them left a two hundred and fifty thousand dollar life insurance policy and I was the sole beneficiary. I'd never wanted to touch the money so I'd left it in a high-yield savings account and over the years the interest had grown. With that money I decided to become an equal partner in Shelley's company.

Shelley turned out to be nothing like the first impression I'd had of her. The tears in her eyes when I presented her with a two hundred thousand dollar check were evidence of that. She wasn't a stuck up phony and she worked just as hard, if not harder, than I did. She was a jokester and thought that all men were good for was making babies, but she was serious about her work and it showed. She was also married and the step mother of three kids. I could tell that there was a story behind that because of the pain that skittered across her face when she mentioned it.

Her eagerness to make the business work rubbed off on me and together we were getting things done so fast that we'd already landed our first five clients. She and I had put our heads together and came up with a list of potential clients that we knew from our previous employers. She convinced two clients from her previous employers to sign on with us and I convinced three from B&G to sign on with us. It wasn't easy. Out of a list of forty we only landed five, but it was a start and they were high-end clients.

The office was a two story plantation-style home that we had gutted and turned into our office. It was in the heart of historic Inman Park and Shelley and I had been busy cleaning, hiring, and sorting things around. She'd decided to take the second floor office for the time being because she didn't want me running up and down the stairs being that I was pregnant. It was weird for me at first being that I wasn't used to that side of the business. I was always the one doing the stuff the execs didn't want to do. At first I was nervous and scared, but as Shelley said, what's there to be scared of when you're doing what you need to do to secure a future for your child? I hadn't gotten around to telling Aric about it yet, had no idea how he would feel about it.

The day had ended and I was at home waiting for Jamie to show up. It could have been my paranoia, but ever since I'd told him that Aric was the father of my unborn child, I felt as if he'd been avoiding me. Jamie and I would have usually talked every day, but my calls had gone to voice mail and my texts went unanswered. He finally answered the phone and I invited him over, more so I could ask him what the problem was. When his black Charger pulled into the drive way, I went to unlock the door for him to let him. As usual, he looked good. His locs were always neatly done, and he always dressed to impress. That day wasn't any different. He was dressed in a pair of dark denim jeans, a purple polo style shirt, and casual loafers.

When he finally got to the door and hugged me, I could sense that there wasn't as much energy as there had been before. I closed the door and followed him to my sofa to sit.

"How've you been?" He asked after he'd sat down and gotten comfortable.

"Pretty good, same thing different day," I answered cheerfully as I watched him.

Although there was a smile on his face, I could tell he was either uncomfortable, or he didn't want to be there.

"That's good. You look good though. That pregnancy glow works for you."

"Thank you."

I didn't say anything intentionally after that to see what would happen and when he didn't show his normal flair like before when we'd usually talk I'd known something was up.

"Okay Jamie, you've been acting weird for a while now, what's going on?"

He leaned forward and rubbed his hands together before answering. "I haven't been acting weird. I've just been giving you your space. You have a baby on the way and I'm sure what's his name has been occupying all of your time."

I folded my legs underneath me and rested my arm on the back of the couch. "No and even if he had been, you can't return a phone call?"

With an exaggerated sigh he turned to me. "Look I don't know if you do this intentionally or not, but you give me mixed signals. I don't know what to expect from you and I don't know what you want from me, but it doesn't take a rocket scientist to know that . . . I'm feeling you in a way I know you can't reciprocate. I like you Chyanne. I like you a lot and I don't know how I feel seeing you pregnant with that man's baby especially knowing how he treats you."

All I could do was stare pointedly at him. I was not expecting him to come out and say that and I was definitely not expecting the attitude that seemed to be in his voice.

"You knew I was pregnant with his baby all along though. I didn't make that a secret. I never knew you felt that way—"

"Because you're too busy chasing after a man that doesn't know your worth."

"I'm not chasing after him Jamie!"

"My bad, you're waiting for him to chase you," he said sarcastically

I had no idea why he'd started to attack me, but it was clear that he was in a bad mood and taking it out on me.

"Look I didn't invite you over here so we could get into a tit for tat argument."

"Why did you invite me over here? Why've you been calling me?"

"Because I hadn't heard from you and I got worried. Is that a crime?"

"It is when you keep playing with my feelings, and don't tell me you didn't know how I felt. Anytime you've called me I've been there. You couldn't even get Aric to answer the phone when you were in the ER pregnant with his child."

I was starting to get pissed. "He didn't know it was his child at the time and you didn't have to come. You could have said no."

He sighed and continued to look at me. "Are you so used to being alone that you don't know when someone is trying to be there for you? You called and I was there for you. I'm tired of always being the afterthought. The person you think to call after this asshole doesn't give you what you want. I told you before that I wasn't going to do this shit."

I sat up to get a better look at him when I said, "I'm not forcing you to be my friend Jamie."

"And he isn't forcing you to be his other woman. You're choosing to be," he said blatantly being sarcastic.

I'd gotten so upset that my legs had started to shake. My nerves were on end and I could feel my blood pressure rise. I didn't know what the hell was wrong with Jamie, but he had me on the verge of being ready to put him out of my house.

"What the hell is your problem?" I asked him as my face frowned in frustration.

He stood and pulled his keys from his pocket. "My problem is you're so busy being blinded by a man who will never love you that you can't see the man standing right in front of you who wants to love you."

"I can't help who I love and I'm tired of making excuses for it! I love Aric and I'm sorry if that hurts your feelings—"

"So instead of being this man's woman"—he spat out as he sternly pointed at himself—"you'd rather be that man's whore?"

Before I knew what I was doing and before I could stop myself I had jumped up from the couch and slapped Jamie so hard that I scared myself! My hand flew to my mouth in shock at the realization of what I'd done. The force of slap forced water to his eyes and after he rubbed his hand aggressively over his face one tear dropped down his cheek.

Once he'd walked to the door and snatched it open he turned back to me. "When he's done fucking you over and you find yourself alone. . . . don't call me."

With that he slammed my door on his way out. All I could do was stand in my front room and wonder what the hell had happened. All I'd wanted to do was sit down and talk to my friend like we'd done so many times before and I didn't understand his anger. It's not like he'd ever come out and said to me that he liked me or wanted to be with me. I was not a mind reader! I didn't even understand why he'd agreed to come over if he held so much contempt for me and my love for Aric.

For the rest of the day, my thoughts were with Jamie. I'd felt so bad for slapping him that I'd tried to call him numerous times to apologize but he wouldn't answer. The image of Jamie's face and his eyes watering made my heart fall to the pit of my stomach. I'd finally left him a long message apologizing to him. I also tried explaining to him once again that I couldn't help that I'd fallen in love with Aric and that I had no idea he wanted to be with me. As I was pouring out my sincerest apology, I had to stop and think about what would have happened if I'd known Jamie had wanted to be with me? What would I have done? Thoughts of actually being with Jamie kept crossing my mind and I didn't know why I kept lying to myself, I did feel something for Jamie. It had been obvious, but I couldn't very well try to be with him knowing that Aric had my heart. It wouldn't have been right.

As the weeks went on, I still hadn't heard from Jamie and I'd gotten tired of calling and tired of being ignored. When the first three weeks of April rolled around and I still hadn't heard from him, I'd given up hope that I ever would again and put all of my focus back into work and preparing for the baby to arrive. Aric and I had been getting along better than we ever had. I mean, of course there were a few disagreements along the way, but not as bad as they had been before. I'd seen him smile and laugh more than I ever had and that brought me joy like never before. We worked well together in preparing for the birth of our child. I knew he'd still been dealing with the issues in his marriage so I tried not to stress him any further. When he told me that he was getting a divorce, my heart almost jumped out of my chest and though I wanted to be excited about what that could possibly mean for us, I held my excitement to myself.

I'd just been about to call Aric, as I was supposed to call him as soon as I left the doctor's office. I'd found out the sex of the baby and couldn't wait to tell him that he would be the proud father of a baby boy. We'd tried to find out weeks earlier, but because of the way the baby was turned we had to wait. I'd gotten so caught up in sorting through the baby's new things that I'd completely forgotten to call. I'd known he would come by after work anyway because he liked to kiss my stomach every night before he went home. I found that by then, anytime I got to spend with Aric made me happy. Whether it was him driving me to a doctor's appointment, or he and I shopping for the baby, it all made me feel like we were connecting on a different level. No, he hadn't told me he loved me, and no, I wasn't hoping he would leave his wife for me, but deep in the recesses of my heart, I was hoping for a chance at a family. I was so caught up in my thoughts of Aric, cleaning, and arranging things in the baby's room that a knock on the door startled me.

"Just a minute," I called out as I struggled to get up from the floor. Being six months pregnant and sitting on the floor was not well thought out.

I made it to the door and looked through the peephole. The person standing on the other side was not who I expected. She'd shown up at my house before unannounced and Aric had gone out to confront her and made her leave.

"What do you want?" I asked through the door.

"I just want to talk. I know I haven't made this thing that Aric has caused between us any better, but I'm willing to sit down and listen to your side of the story now. All I ask is that you allow me to apologize," she explained.

As I stood there and listened to her a part of me was screaming for me not to open the door, but the part of me that felt guilty about being pregnant by her husband made me open the door and let her in my house.

"You can have a seat over there," I told her as I pointed to the love seat.

She slowly walked into my home and looked around. She was dressed in black skinny jeans that hugged her frame, a black body shirt, and black gym shoes as she clutched her purse underneath her arm. I'd never seen her dressed in anything but the best and for some reason her attire gave me pause, but I let it go once she'd taken a seat and looked over at me. She sat on the edge of the love seat as if she were afraid germs would jump off on her if she sat back any further. I wanted to sit but for some reason I didn't feel comfortable sitting so I stood across the room and leaned on the wall. I noticed she kept looking at the ring on my finger and that made me want to hide it from her glare as if it would shatter the diamonds in it.

"What do you want to know?" I asked her as I leaned against the bookcase on my wall.

She removed her sun glasses and her eyes were so red that it was almost frightening. "Tell me what's really going on with you and Aric."

I shrugged. "I don't know what you mean."

"I mean . . . are you guys calling whatever you're doing . . . are you two in a relationship?"

Shaking my head I said, "No. Aric never put a title on what we were doing even before I found out he was married."

"So, you honestly had no idea that he had a wife?"

"No."

"How long were you guys having sex before you found out about me?"

"Almost from the time he took over at B&G. I found out I was pregnant after you and I fought . . ."

She chuckled a bit but it was derived from the anger I could clearly sense in her attitude. "I guess my question for you, Chyanne, is why haven't you left him alone? You know he's married now, why are you still sleeping with him?"

"I can't leave him alone because I'm pregnant. This is his child and Aric will always be a part of my life because of that. To be honest, I've tried to leave him alone, but . . . it's hard to when he is always coming around—"

"Yeah, but why would you continue to give in knowing how much this hurts me?"

I wanted to answer her sincerely but, for the life of me, I couldn't understand why it was up to me to leave her husband alone and not the other way around. If I could leave Aric alone, I would. There were times when I wished he would leave me alone so I could move on, but I knew that wasn't happening, especially not with me being pregnant.

"Stephanie, you always ask me these questions, but why not tell Aric to leave me alone? Do you know how many times I've tried to walk away and leave him alone? He always finds a way to make me come back or make me feel bad about it. If I could leave him alone, I would."

"You can! You just don't want to. You and Aric are both selfish and only thinking about yourselves," she yelled. "Why can't you just go away, leave him alone? Is it the money? I can give you enough money to move away, you and your baby, and start a new life somewhere else."

I looked at her as if she had lost her mind. No way in hell was I moving or taking my child away from his father. The look on her face was shrewd and she looked as if she was so dismayed with me that she couldn't stand to be in my presence.

"I can't just move without letting Aric know where his child is."

"This isn't about Aric! I'm talking to you woman to woman. You will never be enough for him. He will always have to have more." The more she talked the louder and louder her voice became. "Do you know how much shit I've put up with from this man? Do you have any idea what it takes to live with and love a man like Aric? He's way out of your league and the only reason he's still interested in you is because you're carrying his bastard! I've seen it plenty of times before. He's cheated on me countless times. So take the money I'm offering you and do the right thing."

By then she was standing in the middle of my floor and I'd stopped leaning on the wall. We were in a stare down, me trying to process all that she was saying and I was sure she was about ready to snap. It was written all over her face and to be honest she was making me nervous. All she'd said had pissed me off. I'd grown to know Aric and I knew what I was getting myself into. What I didn't appreciate was her insinuating that I wasn't good enough for him and that I was only something for him to play with.

"I think it's time for you to leave," I told her as I pointed to the door.

She just stared at the ring on my finger for a second before shaking her head, snatching her purse from the couch and heading for the door. I heard her mumble something about him putting a ring on my finger and lying to her. I followed close behind her not paying attention to what she was doing. All I wanted was for her to get out of my house, quickly! What happened next was something out of a vague impression from my memory. Before I knew what'd happened she'd quickly turned and with a closed backhanded fist knocked me to the ground. I screamed out and quickly scrambled to my feet as my teeth felt as if they rattled around in my brain. That's when she used a back kick that only Jet Li could have taught her and kicked me dead center in my stomach. Pain abruptly grappled me as I fell into my entertainment system and onto the floor. Tears burned my eyes and clouded my vision as I screamed out and frantically backed away from her swift approach.

Doubled over in pain I screamed out. "Oh God! Please don't do this," I pleaded with her holding my stomach.

"All you had to do was take the money and leave," she said seething in anger as she kicked me again, this time in my side.

I fell over on my back as vigorous anguish tore at my insides. All I could do was pray, pray that she was trying to hurt me and not kill the baby. After the third kick, I simply prayed she would stop kicking me.

"Why couldn't you just leave him alone," she roared out as she tried to stomp me in my stomach.

Fight or flight instinct kicked in and I rolled out of the way. When she kept up her approach and yanked my head back with a hand full of my hair, I stuck my nails in her eyes and tried to pull them out of the sockets. She screamed, let go of my hair, and fell back. That gave me time to quickly stand and balance myself on the wall. I saw her quickly scrambling for her purse and I tried to get to my cell phone lying haphazardly on the floor, but because of the pain I was in she was quicker than me and I found myself staring down the barrel of a silver plated 9 mm Sig Sauer. The breath that I assumed would be my last got caught in my throat and I could only stand there.

"Put the phone down, bitch," she said coolly, her aim never wavering.

"Why are you doing this?" I asked barely above a whisper.

"Because your stupid ass just wouldn't listen. You can't just go around fucking up people's marriages and think there won't be consequences. I asked you over and over to leave . . . my husband . . . alone. I've put up with too much shit for him just to walk away from me, and you just wouldn't back off! Then you had the nerve . . . the nerve"—she spat out bitterly—"to walk into my home with my parents there to tell him he was the father of that thing you're carrying?"

Stephanie looked like something out of a psycho thriller. She was sweating with tears running down her face and slobber sticking to her mouth and lips. Blood slowly oozed from the corner of her eyes from where I'd tried to tear them out.

Before I could respond to her, a gushing liquid splattered down my legs like a water fall and pain like nothing I'd never experienced made me scream so loudly that Stephanie gasped and pulled the trigger on her gun. I dropped to my knees as the bullet ripped my flesh and tore through my left shoulder.

"Help me," I pleaded with her as my body hit the floor. I knew that either my baby or I were not going to make it. Pain and fear overrode pride and I continued to ask . . . plead for help.

She just sat there like she was shocked with her mouth opened half mast.

When I saw that she was too shell-shocked to do anything to help me, I slowly tried to crawl for my phone. The pain in my shoulder and lower abdomen made me crawl at a caterpillar's pace, and once again, she was quicker than me. She quickly scrabbled and grabbed my cell phone out of my reach. I pleaded with her to help me again as delirium took over. My house phone rang and snapped her out of the trance she was in. She jumped over me and I could hear her snatching the phone cords out of the wall and knocking things over.

I quietly lay there crying as life edged its way out of my body. I never thought I'd be killed the same way my father had been killed. The only difference was, my mother had killed him, emptied a gun in him because she couldn't take the beatings anymore, and there I lay with a bullet lodged in me because another woman couldn't take the madness her husband had taken her through.

With the last little bit of life left in me as Stephanie ran past me, picked up her purse, looked back at me one last time, and ran out of the door, I prayed that if a life had to be taken that it be mine. I prayed that God wouldn't take my son's life because of the stupid mistakes that I'd made and I prayed that my mother wouldn't be too disappointed in me like I'd been in her. I hadn't gone to see my mother in Augusta State Medical Prison since she'd been convicted of voluntary manslaughter seven years ago and I prayed to God for forgiveness for my judgments of her.

Aric

"Damn son. I wasn't expecting to hear from you until 'round the next holiday," my dad said and chuckled into the phone. "To what do we owe the honor?" his velvety smooth voice asked next. My dad had a voice that was smooth enough to make his worst enemy trust him and that voice had gotten him in a lot of trouble over the years with women.

It'd taken me a couple of months to decide if I wanted to tell my parents about Chyanne and the baby. It's not like I would have been able to hide it after a while anyway, as I'm sure Stephanie would yell it from the rooftop sooner or later. She and I'd had another argument that morning and before it could take on the makings of a physical altercation, I'd left. I would no longer sleep in the bed with her, had decided against doing that the last time she'd threatened my unborn child. Gabe and I had been talking a lot and he made some very valid points. If I didn't want to be with Stephanie then I had to stop treating her as if I did. I'd stopped sleeping in the same bed with her, stopped having sex with her, and stopped giving her any indication that I wanted to work on our marriage.

"When a woman is desperate to make a relationship work she will latch on to any semblance of hope," Gabe had said to me one day after work. *"So stop giving her hope if you know that there is no chance in hell of you two staying together. . . ."*

Usually I didn't take others advice, but Stephanie had been acting strange and talking about how we could celebrate our next anniversary, but there would be no next anniversary. I knew to try and kick her out of the main bedroom would be a problem so I moved out into one of the guest bedrooms. Since then, I'd been contemplating on calling my parents.

"I just decided to call and see how you guys were doing is all," I replied.

He gave a light hearted laugh that many say I'd inherited from him. "You're going to learn to stop lying to me one day AJ."

Neither my father, nor I were big on talking on the telephone, and talking to him always took me back to my childhood. The fact that he'd called me by the name that only my immediate family called me also took me back some years. I'd come to the end of the work day and decided to phone home before trying to fight rush hour traffic. Rush hour traffic in Atlanta started around four and I wasn't that anxious to get home anyway.

"Sure you're not calling to tell us about the *'fat bitch'* you've gone and gotten pregnant?" He went on to ask.

To hear him call Chyanne that had aggravated me. It also let me know that Stephanie had already called my mother.

"Her name is Chyanne," I told him in a no nonsense tone.

"Chyanne is it? She has a name then . . ."

I could picture my dad standing in the kitchen next to the fridge casually leaning against the door post as we talked. I would bet any amount of money that was what he was doing and probably had his pocket knife out shaving his finger nails while doing so.

"I see Stephanie's already called mom then?"

"That would be correct. I should kick your ass too. That's all I've been hearing about for the last couple of days from Nadine. She wanted me to call and talk to you, but you're a grown man, son and as long as you haven't asked for my advice, I ain't giving it to you."

Hearing my mother's name made the muscles in my jaw twitch and made me wonder just what Stephanie had told her about Chyanne. I wouldn't say that Stephanie and my mom had been close during our marriage, but they had enough of a bond for Stephanie and her to talk about certain things. I'm sure that they'd ripped Chyanne apart and I'm sure my mom had passed judgment on her before even getting a chance to meet her. That's the type of woman my mother was. She had the solution to everyone's problem but her own.

Looking at the time, I began to wonder why Chyanne hadn't called me. She was supposed to have called to tell me the sex of the baby, but I had yet to hear from her. That was the plan since I couldn't go with her to this doctor's visit. I'd been disappointed when we weren't able to learn the sex of the baby on the last visit and she knew how excited I was to know. It struck me as strange that she hadn't called to let me know yet, but my dad clearing his throat brought me back to our conversation.

I sighed and replied, "I'm sure mom has had her share to say."

"You damn skippy, but every time she's picked up the phone to call you, I've hung it up. You don't need her messy ass all in your business either. I done hung up on Stephanie about five times. You would think the knacker would get the point by now," he said.

"I didn't mean to cause you and mom any problems dad, but it is what it is . . . "

"Look, like I said you're a grown man and what you do in your personal life is your business. But do know that wife of yours is a fucking loose screw and you should mind yourself around her. Called here this morning talking crazy and crying. Her and your mother carrying on like two clucking hens calling that gal you got pregnant all kinds of names. After a while I snatched the damn phone out of the wall."

I knew my father and I knew if he said that he'd snatched the phone out of the wall then he'd literally done so. The last thing I wanted was for him and mom to be fighting because of me. I'd seen the way they fought and I knew when my father got angry . . . stuff happened. He was a calm man until you pissed him off. I wiped my hand down my face and leaned back into my desk chair stretching my legs to get the blood back flowing in them. Picking up my phone, I checked it once again to make sure Chyanne hadn't called and I'd missed it. There were no missed calls and no text messages.

"Dad you and mom shouldn't be fighting—"

"Do I tell you what you and your wife should be doing?"

"No."

"Then it would do you good to keep your opinion on what me and my wife should be doing to yourself."

"Dad, all I was saying was that I don't need you two fighting about what's going on with me," I repeated to him.

I heard jingling in the background and knew he was now shaking the loose change he always carried in his pocket.

"I'll worry about that and you worry about telling me about this twenty-five year old you done gone and got knocked up."

I really didn't call my dad to tell him the whole story as it pertained to Chyanne and me, but I knew he was anxiously awaiting an explanation. I gave him a brief, but detailed version of what happened with me and Chyanne and he didn't interrupt much. Every now and then he would ask a question here and there like 'what was I thinking not using protection if I wasn't intending to get her pregnant?', or 'why Stephanie and I weren't divorced before I decided to move on?' I explained to him the same thing that I'd had to explain to Stephanie's father to which he had some choice words, but only after my mother had walked into the kitchen and started to fuss about not being able to speak to me.

While he put me on hold to fuss with my mother in the background I dialed Chyanne on my cell. It wasn't like her not to have called or texted, I thought as I looked at the time. It was thirty minutes after three and her doctor's appointment had been at one. I sent a text message to her after leaving her a voice message telling her to call me. When my dad came back to the phone, I quickly ended the conversation telling him I would get back to him later. For some reason I couldn't fathom, Chyanne was heavily on my mind and I couldn't shake the feeling that the only thing that would keep her from calling was if something was wrong. I'd begun to hope that nothing had gone wrong with the baby and that everything was okay. The thought of anything going wrong with Chyanne and the baby unsettled my nerves and put me on edge.

My cell rang just as I was about to make my way out of the office. It was April. My first mind was to ignore her call, but when the phone stopped ringing only to immediately start again and her name popped up again, I answered the phone.

"Yeah."

"Aric?" The voice was that of a young male.

"Yes, this is Aric."

"This is Aaron, April's son. Mama said to call you and tell you that something's happened to Chyanne—"

My heart rate made haste and felt as if it was about to take a running leap out of my chest.

"What do you mean something's happened to Chyanne?"

I could tell he had been running because he was breathing hard. "The old man that lives across the street from her called mama and said that some lady had attacked Chyanne and that she was bleeding . . ."

Not having time to wait for the elevator, I took the stairwell to the parking deck. April's son was still talking but the only thing I could hear was wind in my ear as I raced down the stairs. In my mind all I could see was the image of Chyanne laying somewhere bleeding and clinging to life. I made it to my car and sped out of the parking deck almost having a head on collision with another car in the process.

"Where is she now?" I asked when I'd finally turned into traffic.

"The police and the ambulance are still at her house. I'm standing outside with mama." I could hear the commotion in the background mixed with sirens. "Mama said somebody shot Chyanne and looked like her house had been robbed."

Hearing that Chyanne had been shot puzzled me as I questioned him about why and who had done it. He had no answer. He could only relay what his mother was repeating to him. I could hear April asking questions about Chyanne's condition and questioning what hospital they would be taking her to. I stayed on the phone as I sped down I-75 trying to get to Chyanne's place. April got on the phone and gave me a better explanation of the things he son had relayed to me. I had questions that April couldn't give me the answers to. I asked her if Chyanne and the baby were okay. She said she didn't know because the police and detectives wouldn't give her any information which only frustrated me more. I found myself stuck in traffic which caused me to punch the steering wheel and curse out in anger. Stephanie kept beeping in on the other end of my phone and I had to ignore her calls so I could keep April on the line. So much was happening at one time that I felt as if I had lost control.

By the time I found an exit so I could maneuver around traffic April was telling me that they had taken Chyanne to Atlanta Medical hospital. Forty five minutes later I was rushing through the halls of the ER trying to get someone to give me any information they could on where she had been taken. In the end I was led down a hall and into a waiting area for the families of those who were admitted with life threatening injuries. The room was small with dim lighting. About twenty sky blue chairs with brown arm rests sat back to back in the middle of the room while six more cushioned chairs sat sparsely against the four tan colored walls. A small flat-screen TV was perched against the wall and a vending machine sat off in the far right corner. I took a seat in one of the chairs that occupied the middle of the room.

All the nurse told me was to wait and as soon as she heard something she would tell me. I'm surprised she even told me that after the way I'd cursed her and every other person within hearing distance. I was frustrated, angry, and I felt lost because I didn't know what was going on. It seemed like hours ticked away as minutes trickled by slowly. My leg shook as I irritably rubbed both hands down my face worrying myself trying to figure out just what the hell had happened to Chyanne. A feeling of dread washed over me as the thought of never seeing her again barraged my mind. I hadn't put in perspective just how much she'd meant to me until that moment. Feelings of guilt paraded through me because I hadn't been there to protect her and my child.

A few minutes later April and her son's came rushing into the waiting area. She looked like she had just thrown on the first particle of clothing she could find and made her way to the hospital. Her hair was not done up like it usually was, she was in sweats and tennis shoes, and she had on no makeup.

"You hear anything yet?" April asked me as he she carelessly tossed her purse in a chair next to me and rubbed her hands together.

She and her sons stood surrounding me with fear and worry etched over their faces.

I shook my head and exhaled. "No, nothing yet. What happened?"

"You guys go sit over there for a minute," she said to her sons and she took a chair next to me.

"Why? I want to know what happened too." The tall one who looked to be close to my height said. "Chyanne don't do nothing to nobody. She's nice to everybody and I wanna know who fucked wit' her."

"Jo-Jo if you don't watch your damn mouth, I'm going to jump up from here and put my foot in it. Now sit down! I know you're mad right now, but don't forget who I am," she said to him sternly.

He stood there and stared her down for a few seconds. The muscles in his jaws twitched before he turned away and stormed out of the waiting room. I recognized the anger and resentment behind his eyes. It reminded me of my own whenever I thought of my childhood.

She turned to the twin boys. "Go get your brother before he ends up sharing a bed with somebody up in here," she told them.

"Hey, Aric if you get to see Chyanne tonight tell her we were here a'ight?" one of the twins asked of me. I had no idea if he was Aaron or Aaden.

I nodded. "I'll do that."

They both nodded and jogged down the hall in the direction their older brother had gone. I watched April as she stood and rubbed her eyes.

"I don't know what happened," she started. "All I know is I get a phone call from Mr. Jerry, he lives across from Chyanne, and he's telling me that somebody done attacked the girl."

"Who attacked her?" I asked her as rage filtered through my body.

"I don't know. He said he went to her house to check on her because he heard a lot of screaming and commotion going on. He said he'd found her lying on the floor with a bullet in her and she looked like she had been beat up."

I shook my head trying to wrap my mind around all that she was telling me because none of it made sense. We both were quiet for a few seconds and by the way April was looking at me I could tell there was something else she wasn't saying or something she wanted to say.

"This doesn't make much sense. Did somebody try to rob her? Was it a random attack?"

She shrugged. "I don't know. The cops wouldn't tell me anything."

"Damn! I need to know something," I belted out in frustrated annoyance.

"Justin told me about your wife attacking Chyanne at the job before." April said after a moment of silence.

I furrowed my brows. "So . . ."

"Mr. Jerry said some woman was running away from Chyanne's house right after all of the commotion and the gun shot he heard."

The reality of what she was saying was starting to sink in. "Are you asking me if I think my wife did this to Chyanne?"

Stephanie was a lot of things but I didn't think she had it in her to shoot anybody.

"I'm just saying Aric. She attacked her once."

"Yeah, it was a physical fight. Stephanie isn't stupid enough to shoot anyone, especially not Chyanne."

I stood up, too annoyed to continue to sit. Stephanie didn't even own a gun. She detested the things. I'd known she'd been acting crazy as of late, but I refused to drape my mind around the possibility that she would have gone to Chyanne's to shoot her.

"How do you know?" April asked with way more attitude in her voice than necessary. "If you're running around here cheating on this woman and she showed up out of the blue and attacked Chyanne before, how in the hell do you know what she did and what she didn't do?"

"You need to mind your own fucking business. Don't try and act like you have Chyanne's best interest at heart right now—"

"I know I've done some fucked up shit to Chyanne, and I know I've been a horrible friend," she said as her posture went rigid with defense. "But that doesn't mean I can't and don't care about her well being. She didn't deserve to be attacked and gunned down in her own home because you can't keep your shit in order!"

"That's comical. You're coming at me like I had something to do with it." My voice had escalated enough for people passing in the hall to stop and look at us.

She sighed and exhaled with a look that insinuated I was trying her patience. "Does your wife drive a red Mercedes Aric?"

Panic and alarm gripped me. "What?"

"Does your wife drive a red Mercedes?" she asked again. This time with more force behind her question as she walked closer to me. "Because if she does Mr. Jerry said that was the kind of car he saw leaving Chyanne's house. That's the car the woman was in. So if your wife doesn't drive that color or kind of car you have nothing to worry about."

I didn't answer right away. I couldn't. What she'd said slammed into me like a head on collision. I closed my eyes and bit down on my lip to smother the curses that threatened to escape my mouth. I should have known that if Stephanie was stupid enough to attack Chyanne once then she would do it again! I said a silent prayer that I was wrong but how else could it be explained that a red Mercedes was seen leaving Chyanne's home right after she was shot? I didn't even know Stephanie owned a gun, if she owned a gun. I fought with the decision of leaving the hospital to go and confront Stephanie, or staying and waiting for news on Chyanne and the baby. My conscience was fighting with my heart and, at that moment, neither was winning.

Five hours later after the doctors had told me the fate of Chyanne and my son, I sat beside her bed side with her hand in mine.

"You okay," Gabe asked me as he got ready to leave the room.

I nodded my head without looking up at him.

"Call me if you need me. I have to go and pick up dad from the airport," he said.

He'd come to the hospital after I'd called him to tell him what was going on. His voice was low as if he didn't want to disturb Chyanne.

They'd put her into a medically induced coma because her injuries were so life threatening and the fact that when she got to the hospital she was already crowning. While fighting for her own life, she went through natural birth to fight for her son's life as well which is why they put her to sleep. She had two broken ribs, one having punctured her lung, and she had a gunshot wound to the shoulder. It had penetrated deep, ricocheted off of her collar bone, and stopped inches from her heart. She'd been lucky.

Now I sat beside her with my right arm in a sling. Pain caused me to flinch with a headache so bad it hurt to keep my eyes open, but I'd refused to move once I was seated next to her bed side.

Five hours ago, after April told me about Chyanne's old neighbor seeing a red Mercedes at Chyanne's house, against my better judgment I rushed out of the hospital telling April to call me as soon as the doctors let her know anything. I'd rushed home, needing to know if my wife had actually done what I was suspecting she had done. See, I was beating myself up, kicking my own ass for the games I'd been playing recently.

Making the drive to home gave me time to think and for some reason anxiety took a strange hold of me. Over the past couple of months since finding out I was going to be a father a lot of my perspectives had changed. I realized that for the longest time I had been a shell of the man that I used to be. I mean, I'd been happy, at least I thought I'd been, but just thinking back over everything, the last few years to be exact, I wasn't the same man I once was. Stephanie had been right in her assessment a while back.

I'd always been the smooth talking business man, but I was trying to figure out when I'd become the man who just didn't give a fuck anymore. When had I become the man who didn't love and cherish his wife and when had I become the man who would lead a woman on just to satisfy my own selfish needs and wants? I guess that my love for Stephanie had hardened me. There's a thin line between love and hate they say and I think it was safe to say that all the love I'd had for Stephanie had turned to hate. I was finally able to admit that; finally able to admit that I'd been doing to my wife what she'd done to me in an effort to inflict the pain on her that she'd inflicted on me. As a kid all I'd ever really wanted was for my mother to love me enough to not hurt me. I think she'd loved my father more though and it showed when her love for him turned into her hate for me. People say I looked, walked, talked, and acted just like the man who was my father. Maybe that's why my mother hated me so.

When Stephanie walked into my life, I'd finally found the love that I'd wanted from a woman. The first couple of years with Stephanie had been the best times of my life because I thought, at the time, that she had loved me unconditionally. I found out the hard way that her love was limited. So once again I found myself on the receiving end of a woman's wrath and once again I was left to try and figure out why. Nobody else had the power to hurt me the way Stephanie and my mother had. Chyanne being there the way she'd been gave me the balance needed in my life and now that she was blessing me with a child it had me thinking about just what the hell was going on in my life.

It was almost dark as I pulled into the cul-de-sac. For the first time parking inside of the garage didn't matter to me. Not seeing Stephanie's car in the garage, I called out to her when I walked into the house and got no answer. I laid my keys on the island in the kitchen and followed the music I'd heard out back to the pool. Stephanie was lying by the pool and I didn't know what to feel as I watched her slowly turn and looked at me.

She looked up and smiled when she saw me. "Hey honey," she crooned.

Even though she was wearing dark sun glasses I could tell her smile didn't reach her eyes. It was a forced smile, one mixed with condescension that overlapped a sneer.

"Took you this long to get in from work?" She asked. "I've been calling you . . ."

I slowly approached her, rubbing my hand down my face as I did. I found myself getting angry at the notion that she'd attacked Chyanne. To keep myself sane and to keep from wrapping my hands around her throat, I chose my words carefully.

"I just came from the hospital," I told her.

My words came out slow and precise. She looked up at me. I couldn't see her eyes behind her sunglasses but I'm sure they were in slits. For a second she opened her mouth as if she wanted to say something and then she closed her mouth and continued to silently stare at me.

"Who's in the hospital? Are you hurt? You okay?" She asked as she stood.

When she walked over to me as if she was really concerned and tried to touch my face I slapped her hand away. She stepped back into a defensive posture and dropped both hands to her side. Rage was tearing me up on the inside eating away at my resolve.

"Were you at Chyanne's house today?"

She struggled for breath before asking, "What?"

"Were you at Chyanne's house today, Stephanie, and don't lie to me."

Standing mute for a second, she turned and walked back toward the lounge chair she had been resting in before. She was in a white tunic that covered a red bathing suit with red stiletto heels, and a big floppy red straw hat. I got tired of playing ring around the roses with her and quickly snatched her by her forearm to bring her attention back to me. She squealed and tensed up and like a scalded cat baring her teeth at me.

"Let me go Aric!"

"Were you at her house today?" I yelled in her face.

With the heels on she stood face to face with me, but with the pressure I had her arm grasped in she was limp and that forced me to look down at her.

"Yes," she yelled. "Now will you please let me go?"

"Why were you at her house?"

"I just figured it was time to hear her side of the story. You never tell the whole truth so I wanted to hear it from her. You know, you have her eating right out the palm of your hand. She's so in love with you she can't see past that fake ass smile of yours. You should be ashamed of your damned self playing with women's feelings the way you do."

I shoved her down into the lounge chair gripping her neck as she fell back. I could see her eyes widen behind her glasses because of the pressure I was inserting into the choke hold. The anger that resided in me was so strong that my eyes burned in frustration. The thought of the possibility that my wife had indeed attacked Chyanne and in turn attacked my child gave me murderous intent.

"Aric," she managed to get out barely above an audible whisper.

"Did you shoot her?" I asked her through clenched teeth.

"Aric. . . . please let go . . ."

"Did you?"

I was so close to her face that my lips brushed her nose when I yelled the question in her face.

She shook her head as she gripped my wrist to try and remove my hand.

"I didn't. . . ."

"Why were you at her house?" I asked as I released her neck but snatched her forward by yoking the front of her tunic in my enclosed fist.

Tears fell down beneath the sunglasses as she looked up at me.

"Why are you doing this? You love her enough to come home and put your hands on me because of her? I'm still your wife Aric . . ."

She was talking but at the moment all I cared about was her telling me if she had been the one to attack Chyanne.

"Stephanie, you'd better answer my question—"

"Or what?"

I shoved her face. Her neck snapped back and she fell violently back into the chair causing it to topple under her. Her glasses fell off of her face and the skin on her hand raked the concrete to try and break her fall. Her eyes were fresh with blood and looked as if she'd taken something to them and tried to dig them out. That told me all I needed to know which only incensed my viciousness. She cried out and quickly backed away from me. I followed her like I was a wild animal stalking prey until she had backed all the way against the brick wall. She threw her hands up to shield her face and begged me not to hit her. I quickly stopped myself and just stood in front of her needing a minute to get my senses back in order. In the mood I was in I was liable to do something that I would regret later. So I chilled and once she realized that I was only standing there, she slowly stood. The blood on her hands leaving prints on the wall as she used it to hold herself up.

"Somebody could get hurt listening to you. You can't just walk away from me, Aric and think there won't be consequences," she said as she sucked her teeth and shook her head. "No sir! I've put up with too much of your shit to think you're just going to walk away from me!"

"Stephanie, what does any of that have to do with you shooting a woman? Why? Why would you do that knowing she's pregnant? Why would you continuously attack her when I repeatedly told you she has nothing to do—"

"Lies," she yelled as she left the wall and stormed up to me. "You put a damn ring on her finger and look at what you just did to me for her! I stood in that house and poured my heart out to you, and what did you do? You left our bed to go and sleep in hers," she laughed sadistically, "Oh no, sir! You will not have your cake and eat it too!"

I'd rushed home just so I could know for sure if she had indeed committed the atrocity against Chyanne and now that she'd told me in so many words that she had, I felt sick; sick to my stomach at the thought of me being the cause of it all. A rush of emotions overtook me and I didn't know what to feel. Shame, guilt, anger, frustration, annoyance. . . . they all had a hold of me. My demons had finally caught up to me, I thought as I stood there and stared in the face of the woman whom I'd once loved. How had we gotten to this point? When did it all change?

Stephanie stood there with the injuries to her eyes looking like something out of the movie 'The Ring' and all I could do was stare back into the eyes of the monster that I'd created. I wasn't taking the blame for what she'd done to Chyanne, but I was taking responsibility for my part in the crime that had been committed.

"Why?" I asked her. "Did you want to hurt me so badly that you would take her life and my child's life?"

"Why would you hurt me like that Aric? Why would you let her keep that baby, knowing what we'd gone through? I love you and you just threw me away like it was nothing! Nothing!"

"Stephanie, I'm not about to stand out here and do this with you right now. I don't know how many times we have had to go through this. All you had to do was let go. You know it and I know it. There's nothing of this marriage left. You're holding on to a memory and I can't believe that you would. . . . go as far as to—"

"I did what the fuck I had to do! Isn't that what you told me this morning when I told I would fight you tooth and nail to make sure it would take years to divorce me? So, I did what the fuck I had to do," she yelled.

"Yeah, well now I'm going to do what I have to do, what I should have done a long time ago."

"What does that mean Aric? Does that mean you're going to love me like you should have done? We could run away together. Nobody has to know where we are. We can start over," she said as she tried to wrap her arms around me.

I shoved her away from me, not believing what I was hearing. It was clear that Stephanie had gone over the edge of sanity and I wasn't sure what was more disturbing. Was it the fact that I was blaming myself for not seeing the signs that she was a bit unstable or was it the fact that I may have indeed had a hand in pushing her over the edge? It was all confusing to me and the more I stood there and looked at her the more disgusted with the situation I became. She'd just stood there and all but confessed to gunning Chyanne down in her home and yet she was acting as if it was no big deal, like it was something that she'd just had to do.

"No, that means I'm leaving and you're going to turn yourself in—"

She dropped her hands to her side like dead weight was attached to both arms. The look in her eyes turned as cold as the longest winter night.

"You're not leaving me and I'm not turning myself in," she said in a matter of fact tone. "I meant what I said when I took my vows Aric. The only way you leave me is if DEATH do we part. We took vows that said for better or for worse and I think the worst is yet to come if you think you're just going to walk away from me and into that bitch's arms. You have another thing coming."

I looked at her as if she had lost the rest of the mind she had left. I could kill this bitch! Anger was overriding my senses at the fact that she had just threatened my life. That's how I felt!

"Are you out of your damned mind? You need to be worried about the prison sentence you're facing and not about us being together. Us being together will never and I mean never happen again! Do you understand that Stephanie? You just shot a woman down while she's pregnant and do you honestly think I would stay with you, even if I'd wanted to in the first place, after what you've done?"

My words came out in a low monotone and I said them so the finality of what I was saying could sink in. It was time for me to do what I should have done a long time ago. I should have left her alone, packed my bags, and got the hell on! I should have never entertained the notion of us possibly working things out knowing that I could never really forgive her for all of the dam-

age she'd done to our marriage. I should have known it
was really over when I started using women to get back
at her for the hurt she'd caused me. I'd used countless
women in an effort to make her hurt when in reality I
was never hurting her. She never even seemed to care
that I had been sleeping with other women. Now that
I thought back on all of the petty arguments we'd had
about the times I'd cheated, none of them had hurt her
as much as her cheating had hurt me. So, in the end, I'd
always played myself because Stephanie, the woman
I'd once loved with every fiber in me, really didn't give
a damn.

Now I was forced to stand in my own home and deal
with the fact that I'd put the life of another woman and
my unborn child in jeopardy because I thought that I'd
finally accomplished hurting my wife in return. You
can call me what you want and say whatever you would
like to about me, but I took no solace in what had happened, and if I could go back to day one and do some of
the shit over, I would.

"Don't walk away from me Aric," Stephanie growled
out as my reality check set in and I turned to leave.

I could hear her moving around behind me, but I
needed to leave. I needed to get away from her and
clear my head. Being near her at that moment clouded
my judgment so it would be best if I just left and let
the chips fall where they may. If and when the police
questioned me, I would tell them the truth as I knew
it. Stephanie's voice kept ringing out behind me as she
called my name repeatedly in an effort to keep me from
leaving.

Then, pain ripped through my back near my right
shoulder as a gun shot rang out. It crippled me, took
me down to one knee as I felt the liquid rush of heated
blood soak my skin and shirt. Slobber fell from my

mouth and I watched as it slowly fell to the ground beneath me. The knuckles on my left hand scrubbed the ground as my arm went limp. I gritted my teeth through the pain, stood, and turned to see Stephanie pointing a gun in my direction.

"I said I love you Aric. That means I can't live without you. . . . and I refuse to let you live without me!"

Two things clicked for me in that moment: One, being that it was possible that I could die at that very moment. The second, was that she had really lost her motherfucking mind. In that moment the woman that I'd once loved meant nothing to me.

My mother had put a gun to my face when I was seventeen and told me to get out of her house. That was after a fight she and my dad had and after I'd told her that the slap she had given me across my face would be the last one. Me standing up to my mother meant her threatening my life. Me finally deciding to leave my wife, for good, meant Stephanie threatening my life. Why, out of all the women I could have been saddled with, did I end up with one who would rather see me dead than to see me happy without her?

"Stephanie . . . put the gun down so we can talk," I said to her in an effort to calm her down.

I was a lot of things, but a fool I was not. It was clear that she was no longer playing with a full deck and I had to do all I could to keep her from killing me and herself.

She slowly shook her head like it was too heavy to continue to hold on her shoulders. "Thought you were done talking? You've never listened when I wanted to talk before. . . . If I can't have you . . . nobody can," she stated. "It's just that simple Aric. What part of that don't you get?"

Tears mixed with the blood from the wounds around her eyes trickled like rain on a window pane down her face.

My shoulder felt as if it was being sawed in half and made my right side feel stiff. I had found myself in a life or death situation and at this point it was going to be either her or me left standing. You couldn't have paid me twenty-four hours ago to believe I would be in this situation. I never thought I would see the day I would have my life flash before me and see my wife aiming a gun at my head, ready to take my life because she felt like without me, hers would end. I never saw Stephanie doing anything like this. She'd shown me that no matter how long you knew a person you never really knew them until they showed you who they really were. I had my faults, but I was not about to shoot a motherfucker, or otherwise, because I was hell bent on having things my way or no way at all.

Without thinking about it, when I noticed a falter in her grip on the gun I lurched my body at her in an attempt to startle her enough to take the gun from her. My reward was a bullet that was so close to becoming a part of my brain matter that it grazed the side of head causing a blinding heat as it scorched my skin. I cursed out in blinded anger as my body hit the ground, glasses falling from my face and crashing to the ground near me.

"See, that's your fucking problem Aric. You don't damn listen!" she yelled as she walked over me with each one of her legs on either side of me, gun still aimed at my face.

With her standing over me and pain causing my head to feel as if it was about split in two, all I could think about was never being able to see my child if he or she was to survive. I was not going to allow her to take that away from me even if that meant I would have to do something that I would regret and possibly get me time behind bars. She would not take my life away before I got a chance to see the life I'd created.

While she squatted over me ranting and raving about how she now had my attention I brought my hand up and slapped her so hard she fell over, stumbling and twisting her ankle before hitting the ground.

She went one way and the gun went another.

My vision was cloudy, body heavy, and head felt as if it was about ready to explode as I slowly staggered up, but I was quick enough to catch her before she could reach the gun that had gone flying.

Sirens could be heard in the distance and for once I was glad to have nosey neighbors. We struggled as I tried to keep her in a hold to restrain her and even though the pain that shot through my body was mind numbing I grabbed a hold of her, shoving her across the vast expanse of the poolside. She went tumbling hard across the pavement hitting her head against one of the stone flower pots knocking her unconscious. My wounds got the best of my strength and by the time the police had come running through my house and jumping my fence to get to me I was laid out thanking God and cursing myself at the same time.

After all of the questioning by the police, the phone calls to Gabe, and me getting treated for my wounds, I sat beside Chyanne, stoic. They were able to save the baby, however; he was delivered at only two pounds and three ounces and although he was in stable condition, he was not out of the woods yet. His doctor had explained to me that because of the stress to him during the surgery and Chyanne's injuries, there were a lot of things that could go wrong with him in the next forty-eight to seventy-two hours. Even after seventy-two hours it was still possible that he would have complications.

I'd almost popped a vessel trying to stop the ache that I felt in my heart and soul, but my walls came crashing down again when I looked at my son through the glass incubator. He was so small that I could hold him in one hand. He was on just as many if not more machines as Chyanne was and there was only so much a man could take. They wouldn't let me hold him but there were two holes where I could stick my hands and touch him. That first touch was surreal and when he started to move around like he knew who I was, I smiled. Against all odds he and his mother had come out swinging. I didn't envision that the first time I would see my son would be looking at him through a glass container, but I was thankful none the less.

As I sat there beside Chyanne, I couldn't even open my mouth and say anything worth saying to her. I felt like shit for bringing this on her. I never meant for this to happen to her, never even knew that it was coming. Looking at her and knowing that I was the cause of all that had happened to her opened my eyes to a lot of things. I realized in that moment that she meant way more to me than I wanted to admit. That's why I kept her around. That's why I wouldn't let her go. In the end, she'd been the only one to give me what I was really looking for. She still loved me regardless of my faults, regardless of the things I'd done to her over the period of time she'd known me.

They only allowed me twenty minutes to sit with her and while there all I could do was hold her hand and apologize for the pain I'd caused in her life both physically and mentally. I talked to her, told her that she'd brought our son into the world and that like her, he was a fighter. I asked . . . begged for her forgiveness, hoping that she could hear me through all of the beeping of the machines that were used to help keep her alive.

Once I stepped on the elevator and I was alone, my part in what I'd caused to happen with Chyanne hit me and hit me hard. The next couple of days would be a blur to me. I would take leave from work so I could be at the hospital with Chyanne and our son as much as possible. She wouldn't be in the induced coma any more, but the pain medicine they would have her on would keep her in and out of consciousness. She would wake up hysterical wanting to see her son and would have to be calmed down enough to be told what happened.

Stephanie would be arrested and charged in the assault on Chyanne. Her face would be plastered all over the news and the many unwanted phone calls would start pouring in. They would keep playing the interview with Chyanne's neighbor, the old man across the street who had seen Stephanie running from the house after he'd heard the gun shot and had run to check on Chyanne. People would go on calling him a hero for his part in saving Chyanne's life. I thanked God for him, because both Chyanne and my son would have died if it had not been for him. Police, news reporters, and children services would invade our lives over the following couple of weeks and I would have to come to a decision on whether or not I would want to keep on the path my life had taken me.

Epilogue
Chyanne

Life has a way of teaching you lessons by choice, or by force and my lessons had come the hard way. The day I was able to bring my son home from the hospital was one of the best days of my life. After what had gone down and all of the drama that ensued afterward, I wasn't sure if I would ever be happy again, but my son—AJ is what we called him—made life worth living.

I jumped out of my sleep when I heard him crying.

"Go back to sleep, I'll get him," Jamie said to me.

I watched through a muzzy haze as he pulled his sweats on over his naked body before going to the rest room to wash his hands and then going to soothe AJ. If you're trying to figure it out, no need. I'll tell you why Jamie is here with me and not Aric.

A month after the incident and after I'd returned home, Aric decided that it would be best if we no longer went the route of entertaining the idea of being together. It hurt like hell, don't get me wrong. We fought about it. I cried, yelled, and screamed, but I should have seen it coming. I'd even kept at trying to convince him otherwise, but six months after I was released from the hospital, after all was said and done, Aric and I were no longer anything other than a mother and father to AJ. I mean we'd been doing things together as mother and father to AJ, but he was different toward me, isolated even.

And, all of that had happened after we'd all gotten on a plane and flown to Long Island so his parents could see the baby. Needless to say, that turned into a ruckus, especially when Stephanie showed up. Wondering why she was not locked away in prison? Because until the trial started, her father had hired her some big-name attorney who was conning and convincing enough to get a judge to allow her to stay out of lock up before and during the criminal proceedings. That woman scarred me for life, not just physically but emotionally as well. I was scared to stay in my own home alone at night. I jumped at the sound of cars backfiring. I even jumped at the sound of thunder and I used to love that sound.

Aric was staying with me most times, or I and AJ would go to his house, but that all stopped when Jamie and I got together. Stephanie had taught me a valuable lesson and that was to never underestimate anyone and to never fall in love with another woman's husband. Although when I first got involved with Aric I had no idea he had a wife, I should have been woman enough to leave him alone after finding out he was indeed married. I mean, I know I was pregnant with AJ and for some reason I'd started feeling like I had the right to love Aric, but it still wasn't right no matter which way you look at it.

Did I hate her for what she'd done? I didn't know. It depends on the day. When I looked at my beautiful baby boy, his head full of curly hair, hazel eyes like his father's, and his smooth buttery caramel skin, I get pissed at the thought of, what if. What if I wouldn't have been able to experience him? What if I would have never gotten a chance to hold his warm body in my arms and feel what it was to love him? In those moments, I hated her. Then, sometimes, I felt sorry for her. Even though people were labeling her as psycho, I felt like under that exterior there were a lot of demons that she'd had to deal with. It was hard to explain my feelings with that.

As I laid in bed and listened to Jamie try to appease a cranky AJ, the rain falling down soothed me as it had always done. I turned when Jamie's shadow in the doorway caught my attention.

His smile was a sleepy one as he cuddled AJ in his arms. "He's not feeling this bottle baby so you're going to have to let him latch on to you for a while," he said in a low and even voice so as not to rattle AJ any further.

Jamie had been a Godsend in my life. I couldn't tell you how much he'd helped me mentally and physically get over the hurt of what had happened to me. Although he and Aric had almost come to blows a while back, once Aric saw that Jamie was a good guy and that he treated AJ as if he were his own son, everything was okay. So AJ had his father in his life as well as Jamie, which was a good thing because they both loved him. Jamie never stepped in the way of Aric being a father to his son and I think he and Aric had established some kind of respect when it came to that. I wouldn't go as far as to say they liked each other, though.

"Okay," I said to Jamie as I dragged myself from the bed.

Between work and making sure AJ was attended to around the clock neither of us was getting any sleep. Taking care of a premature baby was a lot of work. Since AJ was mostly breast fed it was rare that he could go anywhere without me so Aric and I had just fallen into a routine. Aric would stop by every day after work unless he was too tired to do so. Aric was a great father, seeing him in daddy mode always made my heart smile.

Jamie bounced AJ in his arms until I took AJ from him. I slowly paced to the front room and turned on a lamp beside the sofa. Even though AJ was still small for him to be a six month old his appetite was huge. I cringed when he latched on to my nipple and I had to adjust him three times before he got a hold right. Jamie brought in pillows and a blanket for me and sat down beside me. His eyes were red and fatigue was eating away at him, but he refused to sleep if I had to stay awake. I appreciated that about Jamie. He always thought about me, always made everything about me. He showed me that a man could love a woman without the hurt and pain that people claimed always came when dealing with love. He was caring and attentive, always paid attention to my needs and wants. He loved me and I knew he loved me with every fiber in him. He showed it daily, whether it was a card and flowers just because, or a simple text to my phone that said he was thinking about me, he showed me in every way.

And that's why as I looked him I felt guilt; a strong surge of guilt every time I looked at him. Why? Because, to know a person loved you, sometimes more than they loved themselves, wreaked havoc on a person who knew their heart still belong to someone else.

I was still in love with Aric, still desired to be with him, still craved him. At first, I tried, I did. I tried really hard to get over him, and I thought I was until I was faced with having to see him almost every day when he came to see our son. My heart called out to him every single time, and I felt guilty because even though I did love Jamie, I knew that if Aric gave me any indication that he wanted to be with me . . . with Aric is where I would be. . . .

Notes

Notes